Curse of the Fig

Short Stories

Jacob M'hango

Gadsden Publishers

Gadsden Publishers
P.O. Box 32581, Lusaka, Zambia

Copyright © Jacob M'hango

Cover photograph - Ian Murphy

Cover design - Neil Harris

ISBN 978 9982 24 114 4

Contents

For you,
lover of fiction.

The Other Side of Lusaka

I don't think of myself as a poor deprived ghetto girl who made
good. I think of myself as somebody who from an early age knew I
was responsible for myself, and I had to make good.

Oprah Winfrey

You are from *mayadi* – the suburbs. That's where you live,
in the ambience created by high walls whose tops are
festooned with mostly dysfunctional electric wires, where
old men stand guard, and dogs, for fear of infection, take a
moment to analyse intruders before they decide to sink in
their teeth, by which time the burglars would have beaten
up (or killed as in some reported cases) the guards (mostly
unarmed) and the house owners (or tenants as in most cases)
before stripping the house of anything and everything of
value. That's your abode, and you're proud of it because
people from the other side of Lusaka treat you like royalty,
or like you've achieved something great for mankind, or like
the sun rises with you, or like you've never experienced – let
alone known the words – *poverty* and *load-shedding*, or like the
president is your best friend just because you live in *mayadi*.
But, it's fine by you – after all everybody has got to hold their
own, even if it might not exist.

You are on a very old model Toyota Hiace minibus going
to the other side. Everything is both horrific and amazing.
You make to open your small notebook, but you can't because
your right hand is squeezed between your thigh and the body
of the bus just below the partially open window and your left
elbow is embedded between two fatty tummy layers of the
man seated next to you or on you – you don't know which.
You somehow manage to extract your hands and reach for
the small black notebook on your lap. You open it and scribble

in it for a minute or two, making sure to block with your left hand the line of sight of the man in case he can read.

You are in the back of the bus and you think everything is *wrong*: everybody is squeezed, except the boyish driver who's clad in oiled sky-blue overalls (you can tell the colour of it by the unstained patches on it); you pick out a stench (imaginary or not), whose origins you can't tell, dominating the air; the man next to you is in a red vest and his exposed arms are sticky with sweat and he appears to enjoy leaning on you; the song on the bus (in which a local artiste wishes Adam did not sin, we all walked naked without a care for fashion, busts and butts were not anything special, and men spent less money consequently) is too loud but no one complains, as you observe some young and old heads rock to the *noise*; one baby, whose sex you can't tell, of about two years old, is crying for corn snacks and biscuits from other babies while its mother looks away in shame; and the conductor in a formerly white T-shirt and black trousers keeps snaking uncomfortably around the squeeze, time after time accidentally elbowing passengers and rubbing his bottom on some of their unsuspecting faces, who mutter a complaint or curse in reply. It all jumps at you as a piece of impeccably choreographed disaster. You think it's crap, all of it.

As the bus starts to leave town, pressing its way through thick traffic, you convince yourself you have to adapt to all this – everything, after all it's just for a day. And with a hand half-aquiver, you write in your notebook, remembering to shade it.

Thief! My handbag!

You are startled, and your pen almost escapes the space between your thumb and index finger. The woman directly in front of you is touching her head and throwing her hands in the air, and, in her wildness, she slaps the girl next to her across the face. The girl shrills.

What will I give my landlord? Please tell me! cries the woman.

Ba-driver, please stop! Her bag has been snatched, says the man next to you.

Big man, respect yourself! says the boyish driver. You think bag can be found? Are you a stranger in Lusaka? *Kwasila* (It is finished) bag has gone. Be careful with open windows! *Mami* (Madam), just go find new money for your rent.

You people, *ba*-landlord! He'll chase me from the house, she cries.

Imwe mami (You madam), respect yourself. We all have problems here. So stop making noise, just shut up, says one very angry-looking man seated on the left-end of your seat.

Yes, we all have problems here. We have our own problems to mind, other passengers agree.

All of this happens over the loud music. It's so noisy you don't even know how many songs have played after the Adam one. You've decided not to listen to the music. But, there are other kinds of noise throwing themselves into the fray: the woman wailing, the girl complaining about her sore eye, up to eight passengers talking about their problems, agreeing and arguing, while others laugh uncontrollably over the woman's misfortune, seeming quite pleased with her for having provided them something to laugh about (and they laugh with all their energies as though it's years since they last enjoyed a good laugh or as if they are afraid they'll cry if they stop). You observe all this, as you return in slow motion to your notebook.

The girl is over the sore eye, it seems, as she's now consoling the woman.

A meeting chaired by anyone with a loud voice ensues (and it appears to you that everyone has a loud voice). You notice they discuss their problems with passion, and on many counts they do so not with the view to formulating a solution but to revel in, and intensify, the pity party. It doesn't escape you that magnificent is the way they bond effortlessly when they share in talk of their common conditions in their end of Lusaka. You admire their bond, fraternity – even when they disagree on an angle of their shared circumstances, there's an undercurrent of understanding and acceptance. And as their catharses unravel, you pay attention, and, listening over the music, bits of their exchanges stand tall.

We need money for our children's school fees.

They want building contributions at church. I'll stop going there.

Manje mami (Now madam), you want to stop going to church? Well, it's up to you – you'll burn alone in hell!

Aah! No! It's too much *ma*-churches asking for money from us poor people. They should help us also.

Nizoona (It's true).

Hunger will kill us.

What plans does government have for us? The government shouldn't forget us like this – we are the ones who vote.

So, just because you voted you want government to buy you food or to give you school fees? Be serious, don't you know that government has a lot of problems and programmes?

But we are heavily indebted. We owe a lot of people. We need help!

What kind of help? For your own information, government owes a lot of money to other countries and foreign organisations. Government needs help; we must help it!

Ha-ha! Helping government? How can we poor and uneducated people help government? You are out of your mind or perhaps hunger is attacking your brain!

No! *Mvelani* (listen), you can help government in many ways. Just look at the state of the drains – you cried for them, government gave you but you are busy damaging and blocking them with garbage.

No! The issues here are hunger, school fees and unemployment. The problem is government. Don't mention drains; we don't and we can't eat drains.

Ah, let's just accept that we are nothing. And whether our children go to school or not, they will amount to nothing too. Children will turn out like their parents.

It's true! We don't live in *mayadi*.

You think these people should stand up and be counted, throw away their laziness, clear their own drains. Yes, you are convinced they are merely a bunch of complaining illiterates. You miss the bus rides on your end of town: every passenger minding their own business, reading a paper or tapping on their phone screens; drivers afraid to play loud or disrespectful music as they know rights-conscious passengers will react and even threaten to take them to the police; conductors treating passengers with respect because they know there's always a goodly number of future employers on the bus; and buses in good shape with more space on board.

The conductor has the takings in his left hand. He gives every passenger their change, except you. You think he's avoiding eye contact. He looks at you momentarily. You quickly do the money signal with your right hand – fingertip rubbing thumb.

He says, Just wait – I'll give you when I find change.

You are sure he's full of crap because you see he has changed money in his left hand, but you don't want to get into an exchange, not over the music and loud voices. Besides, you aren't in the mood for crap. So, you let it slip for now.

You realise you haven't looked out of the window for a while. So you do and see litter on the road and in the storm drains. You get interested in observing the state of the drainage system and, just like the young passenger said, the cement covers on the drains are broken in many places, with rain water failing to flow over the hills of waste lodged in its path.

You see serious health risks owing to this reckless behaviour. You think sensitisation campaigns have to be conducted by those in authority. You also see rusty tin-roofing on houses whose walls look like a grenade waiting for someone to pull the pin.

Kawalala! Kawalala! (Thief! Thief!)

Mugwileni! (Catch him!)

He's crossing the road!

You plunge forward and hit your chin on the back of the seat in front of you. You realise the bus has stopped abruptly, and, frantically, several passengers are getting back onto their seats. Through the left side of the windscreen, you see the bruised, bloodied back of a man in a pair of ripped, muddied trousers running barefoot across the road, heedless of the threat of vehicles as he runs for his life. In a flash, he looks over his shoulder and you behold, in this very moment, everything about his current state. His face, like his back, is bloodied, but you see past his pain, you see fear: fear that he might be running his last lap before the curtain falls and darkness engulfs him, fear that his life will end before he has any chance to live it, fear that his story will conjure shame and it will be spat on as a result, fear that he will die a criminal's death at the hands of his own people whose unsavoury upbringing and undignified condition he's shared, and fear that no one will remember any of the good things he's done – if any. His manner of running reminds you of Usain Bolt, and you wonder what could have become of this thief had someone discovered and nurtured his talent.

A chanting and shouty group vibrating with rage appears and begins to dart across the road just ahead. The group comprises males and females from as young as a decade all the way to middle-age, with some brandishing metal bars, planks, chains, tyres, and stones. You are sure they are out for blood, nothing less. They appear unstoppable, and their mob psychology reminds you of the film *300*. Still, you think they'll not catch their man unless he runs into an obstacle – one within himself. You start to convince yourself that no experience in the world comes anywhere near the energy, life, and preternatural ability awakened in a human who's looked Death in the eye and even died a little.

Your experience at the Boiling Pot, at the Victoria Falls in Livingstone, storms your mind without warning. It's very hot and you're alone. You're under the boisterous waves, holding onto a rock after which you bring your head up out of the water to inhale. And repeat. Then a monstrously powerful underwater current appears out of God knows where and smashes your forehead against the rough surface of the rock you're clutching, and you feel weightless. You open your eyes, the water is boiling violently around and above you, and it's like you only blinked, but you are aware you've just returned. You have no idea where you are. You're out of breath. Your right foot is caught between rocks. Painful. Then you notice the water under your face has red streaks in it before it boils and turns white. You bring your head up to inhale. The air feels divine; it invigorates every fibre of your being, much like drowning in life.

You're on one of the rocks away from the violence of the water. You look at your foot, it's sore and a little bruised. Your forehead is throbbing and bleeding, feeling like it's detaching from your face. The foot and the forehead don't matter to you now; all that matters is breathing. And so, you breathe – like you're doing it for the first time, feeling life, meaning, and energy imbue your whole being; and you exhale everything inimical to your new-found life, your second chance, and realise no one on earth can take away this moment (your moment), not after having found life in death. You stand up and look across the Knife-Edge Bridge and see the sun fall on rain and split into the most beautiful semi-circular colour spectrum you've ever seen. You breathe.

Pii-pii-pii-piiiiiiiii! The hooting brutally rips you from your breathing and throws you back into the present glum goings-on. You see heads peer out of car and bus windows in the direction of the chase. You imagine that the mob wouldn't catch you if you were the escaped thief.

Yes! *Bazamutibula!* (They will beat him badly!) And when he's between life and death, they will tie him with a chain and dress him in tyres.

Yes, and then they will burn him.

What about *ba*-police?

Uhmmm! Police? Police can't do anything. In fact, *ba*-police will only go there after the guy is dead. *Buju azapeza malota* (The police will find ashes).

Just in case the man neither found life nor learned to breathe – which you find very unlikely – when he looked Death in the eye, you wonder what will become of the young girls and boys who will witness, and most likely participate in, the beating and burning to death of the thief. Will they find life in the death of another? Will they learn to breathe early? And those grown enough to be responsible for their actions, will they become better humans after acting as judge, jury and executioner of the man, or will they morph into a worse version of the evil they seek to remove? You console yourself in the assurance they won't catch him. And so, you breathe.

Grudgingly, the bus resumes its mobility. You doubt if it gets any service at all when it struggles over another mountain of a hump and comes down with a metal-on-metal sound, slamming your sore bottom onto the hard seat. You want to complain but everybody seems undisturbed as they chat away, so you hold your façade of peace. You open your notebook and scrawl in it very quickly.

The drains and tarred road disappear behind you. There are now several tired buildings on the sides of the road blasting

Curse of the Fig

Short Stories

out loud music, and you just know it's from equally tired loudspeakers. You see several drunk-looking men outside the buildings and in the doorways. You read the writings: Veterans' Pub, Hard Times, Dance and Live, Cash Point, and 3 Angels Nightclub. You know this is the famous Nkani Market as you see traders on both sides of the now narrowing road.

There's a midnight-black woman seated on a stool behind small heaps of charcoal, constantly looking around and up, visibly disturbed. You are sure she's praying in her heart for the rain not to come again, not today.

An invigorating smell infuses your nostrils.

There's a girl (you're sure she's a new teenager) turning fresh cobs of maize on a wire mesh over a brazier. The smell makes sense to you now: a confluence of wet mud and roasted maize. Oh, your stomach churns in anticipation and you think a loud growl is ramming across it. For once, you are grateful for the noise.

The minibus approaches the stop like it's breaking down. You see several other similar blue-and-white minibuses, all of them very old models, with engines complaining instead of purring. The blue-and-white makes them look somewhat presentable, but their squeaks, out-of-tune engine sounds, and interiors – you are sure – betray their old-timer status. There's a touch of old to them; and the more you look around, the more everything and everyone here seems to have the touch. Yes, you are sure even young people look old, save for the girl turning the cobs of maize.

The loud song on your minibus is now rivalled by other loud music of different genres from other minibuses, just-arrived and loading, whose doors are wide open. You notice the conversation is swallowed, as passengers alight, heading to their different but similar lives under the same skies.

The conductor stands a little removed, looking into the distance. You approach him about your change. He gives you after so much convincing he didn't give it to you on the bus. He looks disappointed, but you refuse to be judgmental, telling yourself he probably has a bad memory. You move to the other side of the road, where a woman tells you, You are blocking my okra from customers – please move!

You wonder how she knows you aren't a customer. You apologise before you move and open your notebook.

No sooner than the pages touch than the ground starts to shake a little underneath you. There's a noise like of cattle hooves stomping the ground behind the small shops behind the bus stop. It reminds you of your grandpa's farm in Mazabuka, how the weight of a hundred cattle storming out of the pen every morning shook the ground, or you imagined it did. The effect, you think, is the same now. Away from the farm, it reminds you of the man in a race from his own people, a race for his life. Could it be that he's stretched the race this far? It's possible, you think.

There's a small dirt road in front of the minibuses pouring into and across the main dirt road which connects to the tarred road about a half-kilometre in the direction of town. You know the storm is coming from there, a little way before the shops. There's violent running and shouting, you can tell, but you can't shape the whirlwind of voices into anything intelligible. The noise is coming closer, as the compounded confusion of different genres of uncoordinated music issuing out of tired speakers begins to get swallowed up in the combo of whirlwind and earthquake, and any moment now it will materialise and make plain its mystery.

The okra woman has been eyeing you as though to say you're misplaced, for she appears increasingly uncomfortable at your presence, but you can see through the corner of your eye that her attention is gradually drifting to what approaches.

You see the woman behind the heaps of charcoal standing, arms akimbo, elongating her neck in the direction of the small dirt road, and the new teenager is also on her feet, asking questions with her hands, while everybody with loose or no commitments makes for the dirt crossroad, and buses begin to empty as what appears like a small riot continues to inflate at the intersection.

You observe how the okra woman now covers the space back and forth between the crossing and her stock with her eyes. You know she's caught up in debate in her head and wishes she didn't have to watch her stand; the same goes for all those watching from afar. You can almost swear they wait for such moments of drama to find something different and sometimes exciting to talk and laugh about, to forget their own issues, to breathe better, if just for a day. It's their drug, you think, their opium, as they all seem to rush into any sort of happening spiked with even the slightest of dramatic nuance. They could be running into a stampede, to their deaths for all you care. But, maybe these people have the experience to go with the crowd-chases.

You imagine the crescendo of the whirlwind rising to the skies and becoming the grey blanket above; that's your head right now, a murky, noisy place where nothing is still. You inhale deeply through your nose and exhale steadily through your mouth. Repeat. You start to feel calm.

Two eyes crawl from your head to your shoes and back to your head, where they start to burrow through your skull. You turn to look at the woman, but her eyes, seemingly oblivious to the vegetable, now dig into what has become a big riot. Your eyes go there, too, and your ears open wider to try and untangle the cacophony.

Hule! (Prostitute!)

Chigololo! (Adultery!)

Mugwileni! (Catch her!)

We shall teach her a lesson!

Yes! They should stop sleeping with our husbands!

Catch her!

You notice the crossing start to give way, as the whirlwind arrives, in the manner of motorists giving way to a presidential procession, but, this time, the sweeper is a naked woman who's racing ahead of the angry, laughing, cheering and jeering crowd whose members look much the same as the first crowd you saw. She turns in the direction of town, coming down the main road, and you think the chase will flash past you in a moment. But, why has she chosen to come this way? You think if you were her you would have crossed the main road and continued on and turned into the spaces between the houses and perhaps manage to lose the crowd and find a hiding place; then you would see about clothes.

These chasers, you observe, unlike the first crowd aren't carrying anything to suggest they want to punish and kill the runner, they don't seem to want this to end. You see some males, especially boys, run ahead of the woman, look back and watch her like their favourite show on TV, smile and let her overtake them as they run behind, watching and cheering as they do. She can't outrun them, you figure. And then it registers in your head they are probably doing this to humiliate her as they don't seem to want to catch her (and some women, with their *chitenges*[1*] falling, reach forward and slap and pinch her on the back as they please before retreating back into the whirlwind), they want to follow wherever she leads and publish what they say she's done.

Once they pass by you and the okra seller, if the woman doesn't turn in your direction and hope to lose the crowd in the squalor behind you, you're sure they'll get to where the new teenager and the woman behind the heaps of charcoal

---

[1*] Plural for *chitenge*: a sarong-like piece of material that sub-Saharan African women wrap around their bodies, usually left to flow to just above the ankles and tied around the waist to serve as a more respectable version of a skirt. It is commonly worn over skirts and dresses.

stand in wait, anticipation written across their persons, naughty grins marking their faces.

For the first time you really focus on the runner, who seems to be in her mid-thirties, and notice she's naked altogether, without even a leaf to cover the meeting of her thighs. Disgrace. Has she got her comeuppance? As she gets nearer to you, you start to imagine with every bounce of her pendulous breasts that she's asking for help. And, indeed, she fixes her big eyes on you. In them you see not fear but shame – a kind of death. That she's already dead you think explains why the crowd is not after her life. It's like she's lived her life and all she wants is a dignified end.

Her eyes again. Is she asking for help or simply willing you out of the narrow opening to the area behind you? Three metres. You think to make way. Two metres. You start to move closer to the okra seller, who doesn't seem to notice you move. One metre. The naked woman turns and brushes past you, almost knocking you to the ground.

The okra seller, like she's protecting her own life, quickly starts to sweep the small heaps of okra into a basket she holds with her left hand; you help her sweep the okra successfully before the crowd knocks your end of the stand to leave it crooked. Luckily, no one is hurt and the okra is safe. The woman looks flustered in her well-fitting blue *chitenge* dress, and you imagine her brown headcloth getting tighter around her head as though to veil her thoughts from you. As she curls her full lips and rolls her small eyes in gratitude or confusion or anger, you think she's a quietly comely woman. You suspect she's soon going to a kitchen party or wedding because she doesn't strike you as dressed to spend the day behind heaps of okra. You both look on as the naked woman and the whirlwind disappear into the squalor.

Thank you, she says.
It's nothing, you say.

Your eyes take in the roasting maize, the heaps of charcoal, and *michopo*[2†] braaing near the buildings' entrances with the drunk-looking men standing outside and appearing to be staring in your direction without a clue of what just happened. You imagine the maize and *michopo* swallowed up in the crowd, the charcoal crushed in the brutality of hundreds of differently shaped feet meeting the ground and the drunk-looking men getting drunker-looking with every push and shove, at least before they fall to the ground and pass out. You're glad the whirlwind took a different course.

Then your thoughts race back to the naked woman whom you hope desperately will lose the crowd and save some remnants of her tattered dignity. Did she commit adultery alone, for where is the man, the married man? You think he should have been sweeping the road with her, and he should have been in front of her because you're sure he initiated the adultery and her role was only to submit after a long period of trying to reject him; her pendulous jugs should have followed him closely behind as he dangled something to his arrant humiliation. You wonder why the stupidity of men is so downplayed while women so often bear the brunt of this stupidity. Who even decides these matters? Who decided a man could do no wrong? And the angry women, shouldn't they be dealing with their husbands? Can't they see the naked woman is probably only a victim like themselves? It infuriates you to think they couldn't even use some of those falling *chitenges* to cover the nudity of their fellow woman and that every time the boys see any woman, irrespective of how very dressed she may be, they will remember the naked woman

---

[2†] A popular local dish of small pieces of chevon, and sometimes of beef or pork. (Its popularity, it must be admitted, is mainly around beer halls.)

and all women will be naked in their eyes. Your notebook is already beginning to feel heavy but you open it still.

You say bye to the okra seller and find a narrow way around the shops. You're now in a much larger area where the arrangement of stands is almost circular. You notice there are more small shops behind the stands. And unlike the seller outside, these vendors treat you like a customer – a real customer.

Please buy my cabbage, it's fresh.
Tomatoes. Buy my tomatoes, they are very big and round.
Onion.
Rape.
Chinese.
Kandolo (Sweet potatoes).
I beg of you. Please buy.

Their pleas make you feel guilty just for entering here. Your being here is the heavens opening and showing them their salvation in a teasing manner. These women want their salvation today. You observe they look like they've endured many broken promises and they want none of it. If you buy from one, you know you'll have to buy from all of them (not entirely true, but you feel like that); and if you say you'll buy from them later, it will be a broken promise before you even complete the sentence. So, you turn back the way you came and sense more than see the deflation on their faces, sighs of resignation. Once outside, just in front of the shops, you open your notebook, before you amble to the minibuses.

You are determined to avoid the squeeze this time. So immediately a boy jumps into the front seat, you jump in after him and shut the door to the visible utter chagrin of the man who clearly shared your strategy. You don't care. You roll down the window and rest your elbow on the door, notebook in hand. You're comfortable. Your watch tells you it's a little past noon.

The thirtyish-year-old driver, you observe, looks clean in his navy trousers and sky-blue shirt, and as you leave the station you're surprised the bus isn't noisy and there's no stench. How is this possible?

The radio is on and it's news hour, but you're sure the sound isn't reaching the people in the back. There's no conversation; you turn your head to see if the bus is full, and you inadvertently lock eyes with the peeved man in the back, right-end of the bus. His eyes burn with anger, yours with compassion. The bus is full. You return your eyes to the front and look through the windscreen.

As you pass the braai stands, and as tarmac appears in front of you, something you never could have thought possible happens: your notebook is snatched from your hand just when you're about to make an entry. It happens so fast you think only the boy has noticed. You didn't even see the body to which the big hand was attached. But who could have the uniqueness to steal a notebook in this place, while other snatchers aim for phones and handbags? You wait for someone to pick up on it and spark conversation but no one does. And you think it's ironic that the sun has chosen this moment to start peeping through the grey and reassert itself.

You console yourself it's not a big loss as you remember what you wrote and can easily re-enter it in another notebook. You're confident you'll be better for it after your experiences today than when you started writing. You were making entries under the title *The Other Side of Lusaka: Perception vs. Reality*, and some of your last entries loom large in your mind. There's no way you're going to forget them.

– free in a way that transcends boundaries

– enjoy true cooperation, working together to root out from their communities what they deem unacceptable behaviour, by any means necessary

– rarely smile and laugh, just like in *mayadi*, but when they do it's as pure as snow and bright as sunrise / no snow and sunrise in *mayadi*

– may be poor (and they don't hide it), but they are rich (very rich) in ways *mayadi* will never know / the *mayadi* poor die alone / to be elaborated

–more resistant to shocks because of their support system / to be elaborated

– the women are very beautiful / discovery needed

– just like everyone else, they have problems and issues

– the view from *mayadi* is mostly a matter of flawed perception / spend time with them, know them

The boy glances at you again. In his flip-flops, khaki shorts, and a yellow short-sleeved shirt, he looks smart and calm. You think he should be in school, you guess Grade Five, and his friends must be in class now. But, he could well be one of the many children not in school in this place, you conclude, maybe a child of one of the earlier set of passengers.

You're on the tarmac and the minibus complains as it struggles over the menacing humps when you see several groups of people in what appears to be serious conversation by the roadside. They are audible enough now, and you (and you're sure other passengers, too,) pick the gist of the conversations.

Bamupaya (They've killed him).

Ah! *Bamushoka?* (They've burnt him?)

Yes.

The rest of the way to town is a blank. You return to transact with the conductor – you aren't here except for your body. Why did he let them catch him when he knew what awaited him at their hands? Didn't he taste of the enchantment of life when he looked Death in the eye? Or, did he even look Death in the eye? On the whole, you are transformed, renewed, reborn – and confused. You come back, ready your pen, but there's no notebook.

Curse of the Fig

The heart is deceitful above all things, and desperately wicked:
who can know it?
Jeremiah 17:9

I'm one of many standing under the heavens that promise a rainstorm, most likely a violent one that will come soon or later - or not today. Largely oblivious to myself, my mind drifts as dazzling lightning signatures zigzag across the deep-grey canvas above. What are they trying to say? Tears burn my eyes and toss me back to the moment, a glum moment

The prophet's mouth opens and begins to drip with consoling words that sound like a canticle, to try and raise my spirits. (It does this in a way that makes me think it must have swallowed the Blarney Stone.) The bearded mouth of this middle-aged prophet knows exactly what to say to fit any situation under the sun. It said when she still had the sparkle of life in her eyes, that this was her year of harvest and that we would grow old together.

She and I won't celebrate our fifth wedding anniversary tomorrow, because she won't be available.

II

Our last anniversary was simple and fun-filled: Martha, Michelo, and their husbands (Vernon and Musa, respectively) in attendance, our house warmed up with their laughter. She and I often marvelled at how her two best friends' names started with M. And when with them she would introduce herself as Mendy to complete the M-triangle. She always insisted on it, 'Call me Mendy. Mendy.' And they were very good friends; they kept going strong from their childhood – secondary school and the University of Zambia together, that sort of childhood. It didn't matter that Martha studied Medicine, Michelo Demography, and Mendy Economics; they seemed as close as ever. Martha was almost our official family doctor, and we always got preferential treatment whenever we visited the University Teaching Hospital (UTH), the last being a year ago when we could have sworn upon our beating hearts that Mendy was pregnant. And when it wasn't to be, we were back to being just fine – our shock-absorbers had learned to handle the glaring rut of the thankless attempt at trying to get back at talkers.

'Aren't we having fun!' she exclaimed, as she began to get tipsy on the champagne, her smile alight. Vivacious. She was sunshine and warmth lodged in a petite body. A sylph in my eyes. I liked to think of her as a diamond filled with light. The brightest of them all.

Admiration tinged with acceptance permeated the air when I recited to her my new poem to the tune of Enya's 'Shepherd Moons.'

> It gives me life measureless,
> And fills me with myriads of joy.
> It dries all my tears,
> And blows my fears away.
> You beam a light into my darkness,
> As we walk this love isle.
> What then is brightness,
> If it be not your smile?
>
> Put side by side with the firmament,
> More beauteous would be your face.
> My fingers itch to touch your aspect,
> The expression of perfect feminine grace.
> As water is the ocean's specialty,
> So is your aspect's specialty fairness.

What then is beauty,
If it be not your face?

'Way I would have made them,
They stick out proud and glossy.
Red grapes and strawberries grow on them,
And they drip with milk and honey.
The sight of them drives away emptiness,
And a virgin page flips.
What then is sweetness,
If it be not your lips?

If He made me recreate you,
You would come out the same.
As I would not make anything new,
Alteration would be to my shame.
For He set out to redefine architecture,
When He likened you to nobody.
What then is structure,
If it be not your body?

I know what it means to be blessed,
For He gave me an angel to love.
That I be forever pleased,
In a love that no one can move.
In all His creational thought,
From where you came,
I dare doubt it not:
God thought of me.

Later, in the bedroom, luscious in her racy black
nightgown, she said to me, 'Look at us.'
   'Yes?'
   'Look at us!'
   'Yes, I heard you the first time.'
   She then played me Vince Gill's 'Look at Us,' looked me in

the eye, brushed her full lips against mine and French-kissed me with abandon. I ran my fingers through her hair, as our tongues wrestled. It felt like the first time. Perfection. Soon we were lost in the access of the pinnacle of marital bliss, where the material world dies and a slippery link takes over.

The morning came crusted in gold. Golden rays streamed in through the bedroom window, ushered in by the early morning sun. They danced on her silky skin, her eyes sparkled, and her smile rivalled the light. It was the smile of a goddess reserved only for me. We would often say to each other – and believed, I guess – that albeit every next morning was fresher and newer and seemed to gleam on everything, our love was fresher and newer than every morning and its gleam upon us was unrivalled.

'Honey,' she said, her face immediately veiled under an anxious cloak of mystery.

'Yes, love?' I responded.

'May I ask you something?'

'Yes of course! Since when do you have to–?'

'Well, do you believe in Nietzsche's thought that whatever is done for love occurs beyond good and evil? That love is all-powerful, and therefore it follows that it can't be categorised?'

'You mean, um, the way lying for love transforms the lie from black to white? Something like that?'

'Yeah. That sort of thing.'

'Well, I guess I do, um, to the extent that it's reasonable. Um, yeah.'

She looked at me like she was looking for some clue of some sort. 'Honey.'

'Yes?'

'What would you consider unreasonable?'

III

'Hold her! Somebody hold her!' the prophet's mouth cries.

And just in time she's held and restrained from throwing herself into the hole that to me is bottomless, an abyss that swallows and never spews out, a lonely channel, one of many through which those whose hearts no longer beat leave this earth and go to join the spirits. I want her to be swallowed.

Her eyes are bloodshot behind the tears that soak her face and black cotton blouse. Her black *chitenge* and brown pumps are muddy – the red mud has dyed her waist-down. She sits in the mud near the hole, waiting for a lull in attention on her to have another go at her antics. But she can't be ignored as she's the loudest wailer. She seems to be doubly bereaved, and one can tell, among those who know her, that she's mourning the loss of her family: husband and daughter. She sobs hard, and asks, 'God why? Why?!' A clear thin stream of snot runs down her lips (that now seem swollen like her every facial feature) to her chin, forming slimy strings stretching to her blouse. She looks tousled, her locks dishevelled, and it's immediately clear that she's crossed fifty.

She's a famous farmer in Lusaka, supplying carrots, cabbages, yellow and red peppers, onions and tomatoes to Shoprite, Pick n Pay, Food Lovers, Spar, and the Soweto marketeers. They call her 'Umaga.' She's thickset but seems to have no problem carrying her weight. Some say she has the strength of an elephant, and this shows every time those six seemingly strong male farmhands struggle to keep her from jumping into the abyss. I think she has the strength to take them with her if she wanted.

I feel sorry for her, but I want her to disappear, to jump into the hole and never return; for she's a reminder and restorer of betrayal and pain. I wish she'd died of depression (or something related – even unrelated) two years ago when her white farmer husband, who was in his late seventies, died in his sleep. I liked him; he was avuncular and fully accepting of me as his son-in-law; and, unlike Umaga, he never once treated me as inferior. Rumour holds that she killed him. They say she did so to remain in charge of their 200-hectare fully mechanised farm.

She swore to Mendy and me, at our third wedding anniversary party, that it was just a rumour – nothing more. 'Be not swayed by the rumour,' she said. 'You know Keith and I were married for many happy years that I wish I could rewind. I loved your father, baby.' She always addressed Mendy as baby.

We believed her. 'We know mum,' Mendy said. 'We can't begin to think so low of you. I know how much you loved dad. So, forget the rumour…let's celebrate!'

And how she mourned her husband! Now she's here, tormenting me, making me a public joke.

'It is appointed unto all the living to die once, and then the judgement!' the mouth declares loudly, punctuating all the mourning songs that can be heard from other choirs attending other burials in this Leopards Hill Cemetery, as if to get everyone's attention. It has worked as Umaga's hard sobs now ebb into mere body jerks, her eyes dart between the epitaph bearing 'Keith Martin' and the hole, our 'Nearer My God to Thee' comes to an abrupt halt, and their 'Kumbo Takuya Babwela' (those who die don't return), 'Kalombo Mwane' (yes Lord), 'Mubili Wangu Mbulongo' (my body is soil), and 'Chalo Chamaluba-maluba' (world of flowers) seem to have taken a knock before they recover.

'The Lord gave. The Lord has taken. We will be foolish to refuse to remember and celebrate the life of our dear departed – a beautiful angel whom God himself has required more than we do. She was a selfless soul who gave abundantly to the cause of the gospel, for she desired for many others to be saved, to come to the saving knowledge of God.'

A signature flash rams across the skies in what seems to be approval, and ear-popping thunder follows. Everybody shivers a little, including the prophet, but not Umaga who's in her own world. She rocks a little – backwards and forwards – to a tune that only she can hear. Her body jerks no more. I've been willing her to make eye contact with me, but she won't. I don't exist in her world.

'Some of you will remember that…that…I said early this year, in January I think, that this was our sister's year of harvest, and you might be wondering: "Why this? Was the prophet wrong?" The prophet of the Lord is always right, knowing the perfect will of God, understanding His mysteries, and seeing beyond the farthest reach of the human eye.'

At this point there is a chorus of several throats clearing in the choir section and an uneasy shifting in the crowd of mostly black-clad mourners. I zoom in on the prophet's face, trying to see if those eyes will look at me – they dart everywhere but in my direction; in fact, they haven't looked at my face today.

'There is no event that makes the Lord happier than when one dies in Christ. The Lord and the entire heavenly host are overjoyed to welcome our sister to paradise. Funny thing is that, she is not happy that we mourn her passing; she wants us to celebrate her entry into Glory Land. For when we say goodbye, heaven says welcome! In my deep wisdom given by God and inspired by the Holy Spirit, I saw our sister in paradise walking on streets of gold with the angels. One moment she was walking on air, another she was soaring in the skies like an eagle and she wore a starry crown and a robe whiter than the whitest. The vision kept coming back to me every time I prayed. I asked the Lord why. He then told me to declare in church that this was Sister Wendy's year of harvest; and obediently, I did. He told me that the real life of a seed is in its death. And let it be known that Sow a Seed Miracle Church thrives upon that very principle.

'Beloved brethren, remember the words of the Apostle Paul: "For to me, to live is Christ and to die is gain." Now let me describe where our sister is: it is a twelve-gated city, each gate guarded by an angel, the walls made of jasper, and the city of pure gold. Trust me, the gold of this world is nothing but charcoal. Hallelujah!'

'Amen!' the mourners agree.

Fired up, the prophet looks at me, gazing at my face. 'And the foundations of the wall of the city, where our sister is now, are garnished with all manner of precious stones: jasper, sapphire, chalcedony, emerald, sardonyx, sardius, chrysolyte, beryl, topaz, chrysoprasus, jacinth, and amethyst. Brethren, some of these stones do not exist in this world; they exist only in paradise. Each of the twelve gates is a pearl, and there is no sun there for Christ is the light. And if you must know brethren, Christ shines brighter than the sun. That is where Sister Wendy is right now and will be for eternity!' he says, a wide smile marking his face.

I find myself yearning for paradise; to walk where she walks, to fly like a bird, but how would I react? Just in time, I hear, 'There's no heaven here; she was a –.' The sudden shuffling in the crowd swallows the last part of the sentence. It's immediately clear to me that they are judge and jury, and they have already passed the verdict – and they're right. All this coming together and singing and looking sorrowful is a farce. But I wonder if the prophet believes in the beautiful, vivid celestial picture he's painted. I want to believe he believes.

As opposed to the sharp, loud clap, there's an extended, low rumble as the heavens darken menacingly. Something is certain to burst up there. And to think that this duskiness is closer to the beauty so eloquently described by the prophet. In truth, I find it reassuring to think of paradise looking downwards than upwards, and that is the irony as everyone only half-glances at the sky, a now unappealing, uninspiring, unwanted cover, a disruptor of human affairs.

'Man looks at outward appearance, but God looks at the heart. This is to say, brethren, that while people judge actions, God judges intentions. There is a lot we do not know, but God knows and sees everything. Judge not that you be not judged!'

Everybody is quiet and perfectly still now, waiting to see if the prophet will dare step into the murky waters of the debate around her final days on earth. They listen with bated breath. But the prophet, in what seems to be his deep wisdom given by God and inspired by the Holy Spirit, deviates from the mud.

'I know that my Redeemer lives, and at the last He will stand upon the earth. And after my skin has been thus destroyed, yet in my flesh I shall see God. She is with God. She is looking at Him right now. I see her, I see her!'

I want to see her, too. I want to know if the prophet has seen God. And everybody gazes up at the black menace, squinting and widening their eyes repeatedly, patently willing their eyes to see what the prophet sees. My pupils dilate and constrict to no avail. Then, an epiphany: *He hasn't addressed our growing old together. How can he possibly explain it away?*

IV

Ten days ago, she left for Livingstone to attend a workshop on organisational restructuring (that is what she told me). I do not know the full details as she did not divulge them all, and I did not ask. It was her fifth workshop in Livingstone this year. As manager for Proflight's Lusaka branch, she was flown there and was to be flown back after five days.

On return day, she said she would instead be driven to Lusaka as there was still some business to discuss with two Saudi Arabian partners who were scheduled to remain at Mazabuka.

I waited. And when I received a call – the call that would change my life for ever – from the police asking if I was her husband, my heart twirled and repeatedly attempted to break my ribcage, my throat lost all its moisture, and I was lost for words. It took me about a half-minute to finally respond to the police officer, who'd kept saying, 'Hallo, are you there?

Are you there? Stop wasting time *ya boma ka!* Tell me, are you the husband?' He quickly sounded conciliatory, warm and formal when I agreed. 'Sorry, we assumed the gentleman with her was her husband, but we found she used a different surname. I rummaged through her phone and found your contact saved "Hubby Mateka." I alerted the senior officer in charge of the case and he authorised me to call.'

'Off-off-officer, what are you talking about? You're using my wife's phone…give it to her, let me talk to her. Please!'

'Oh…sorry Mister Mateka. Mister Mateka, right?'

'Right.'

'Let me start from the beginning. Oh, before I do I need to ask you some questions if you don't mind.'

'I mind. Just tell me what the hell is going on!'

Musa looked at me and his face asked why I looked shell-shocked and yelled so into my cellphone. I had nothing to say to him; there was nothing to say.

'Okay. Hold on sir. Superintendent Hambweke will tell you more. Hold on!'

I had questions. Many of them. Jumbled. The gentleman–? Why–? It dawned on me that, for some reason, I couldn't phrase the questions. It was definitely going to be wise to wait on the police officer to talk while I, like a dry sponge, soaked up every bit of the information. The wait was insufferably painful, an eternity that spanned a minute.

'H-h-hallo…hallo! This is Superintendent Hambweke calling you from Mazabuka Central Police Station. You were talking to Constable Malowa. So, Mister Mateka – I am sure that is your name; that is the one we found – what exactly did Constable Malowa te…tell you?' he drawled.

I wanted to stretch my arm through Chilanga, Kafue, and the Munali Hills all the way to Mazabuka and strangle the retard, but not before squeezing information out of him. I could picture him: threadbare head (if he had any hair at all), paunchy, stubby-nosed – and obviously drunk, for he sounded lazy-tongued.

'Hambwe…officer, with all due respect eh, what the hell's going on there? Where's my wife?!' I felt suspended above my sofa, weightless, grasping firmly – firmer by the minute – onto the phone as if it were a wily animal holding a world record of escaping the tightest of grips.

Musa looked at me, concern chiselled on his face, mirroring the state of my person. He empathised. And he, too, seemed to have sensed the obnoxiousness of what was bound to come from the South; he shared in the sense of knowing that had now infused the air between us, brought on by the wily animal in my grasp.

On the TV, commentators commentated, players played, goals were scored – inferring from the spectators' celebratory noise, cheering and booing – but we would have none of it; we looked but saw nothing of the football match.

'O-O-O-Okay. Mister Mateka, let's take it easy. Tell me, where are you right now?'

'Home.' I tapped on the speaker icon.

'Okay. Are you with someone there?'

'Yes.'

'Who…who are you with?'

'Officer, just tell me. Please!'

'Sorry sir, it is…it is called Standard Procedure. Just answer my questions. They are not–.'

'Fine! I'm with a friend…a male friend.'

'Okay. In that case… according to eye-witnesses, two hours ago an over-speeding blue Toyota Fortuner detoured from the road and hit into a tree. That was after overturning three times. We were at the scene of the accident approximately half an hour later. And registration number…ah… Well, I need to look at it again.'

I glanced at the wall clock. Three minutes past seven. A Saturday evening gone awry.

Having heard the conversation from 'Standard Procedure' to 'blue Toyota Fortuner' to 'I need to look at it again,' Musa's eyes widened in disbelief. He said what was on my mind, as if to himself, while nodding, 'Vernon. Yeah. Vernon's Toyota. But, he's supposed to be in Ndola since four days ago.'

I hoped against the evidence this far, until the officer came back with the vehicle registration number. I was utterly devastated, and I did not know how to feel when he said, 'I am very sorry, but the lady died on the spot. The gentleman, a Mister V. Likezo, bearing a ZESCO Senior Electrical Engineer's ID, is in a coma. He will be at UTH before midnight.' There was now no doubt I had been screwed over. And how dare he called them lady and gentleman. I now had a cornucopia of questions for them, but they would not speak or look at me. I was in a trance. I felt nothing – not space, not time, not life.

Musa was the lead character in the film I was watching. He grabbed the phone and got so busy speaking into it softly, at times in whispers, with a most consoling expression on his face. Repeatedly, he would look at the phone screen, tap-tap on it like a madman, wear the mask of someone looking for something, then wear the joy of someone who'd just found something; and with a complete shift in form and manner, open and close his mouth unremittingly, nodding or shaking his head as he did. He acted adroitly in an interminable film. At one point he shook his head violently and jumped out of the film momentarily to tell me the funeral would be at Umaga's farm; his words were a slur, but the meaning was clear. He was back on the phone: opening and closing his mouth, nodding and shaking his head.

V

Something with dark wings and a white chest perches in a nearby acacia tree that sways in the howling wind: a Black-shouldered Kite. I'm sure it's observing me; I don't know why but it is. Has it come to commiserate with me? Does it understand what's going on? Does it know the pain of loss mingled with betrayal? Has it ever loved so hard and lost so mercilessly? Will it ever know what it's like to be human? Oh, I wish I were a bird! I would play in prickly trees and not get hurt, I would experience the freedom of flying without a care in the world, I would soar high in the sky above deceit and sing birdy songs of uplift, unlike these gloomy songs of humans – these two-faced humans whose intentions are a cauldron of bedlam in which death rankles and waits. If only it were my friend! It would teach me to fly, sing, live with abandon, go anywhere I wanted, do whatever I wanted, and in utmost disdain for them, shit on these people. I look at it, it stares at me. Does it know my thoughts? Does it want to be my friend? I have an eerie feeling those small deeply-red eyes have the power to see through me, into my soul, and maybe they're already weighing my worth as a human. So, I stand before this bird and it judges me; its eyes have no regard for my clothes, making me feel naked and exposed. The sight of it begins to irk me.

I shift my gaze to Umaga. There she is: rocking no more – perfectly still.

The Soweto boys rush for shovels, ready to fill the hole. Three soil-carrying shovels circulate among mourners. One shovel comes to me, I dip my hand into the damp, red soil. I feel disappointment and anger course out from my being, through my arm and hand into the soil. My voice can't carry this mass of emotions to her, so I pin whatever ounce of faith I have on the soil taking my message to her. I imagine that as the mahogany coffin gives way and maggots and worms have long since invaded her body, this bit of soil will make contact with her rotting flesh and as it becomes soil, there'll be no telling between this soil and the soil she becomes. Then, I'm certain, she won't only understand but also feel the full measure of every atom of my pain and shame.

The Soweto boys begin to drop loads of soil into the hole to the repeating tune of 'Nearer My God to Thee,' as the prophet continues to crackle over the sombreness. One of those Soweto wheelbarrow pushers, who somewhat carries himself

like their leader, shouts at a seemingly hung-over friend, '*Iwe,
don't be lazy – tiye fwikila!*' Animated, the malnourished-
looking one pushes his body too far; he slips and looks ready
to fall in, but his friends' nimble hands grab him. The shovel
– alas! – escapes his grip and I think I hear metal on wood.
Gasps fill my ears.

As they resume dropping loads of soil into the hole, I
imagine Mendy's body broken, swollen, mashed-faced, and
unrecognisable. Do they even know what they're doing?
They seem to be enjoying it. In truth, they're locking away
my sunshine and my shame, my pleasure and my pain, my
laughter and my tears, my breath and my suffocation – my
life and my death. They're interring a contradiction.

My tears have dried. I'm in a place beyond right and
wrong, good and evil, life and death. I feel nothing human;
indeed, I feel immortal.

A nudge from my left; it's Musa. I realise that he's been by
my side all along. I look at him vacantly. He whispers, 'The
wreath. She's handing you the wreath.' I can't lift my hands
to touch it. He takes it, eases it gently into my hands and
walks with me to a mound of earth.

The prophet begins to crackle what sounds like a
motivational talk directed at me, as the choir begins to sing
'Chalo Chamaluba-maluba.' We squat at the head of the
mound and deposit the brightly coloured wreath of orchids,
lilies, and roses. My instinct is to stand up and get back to
where I was before. I make motion, but Musa holds onto my
hands firmly under the rich colours and mishmash of sweet
smells. 'Pay your respects,' he whispers, and nods his head as
if in prayer. I follow his cue. And soon we are back, standing
and staring, as Umaga takes a wreath to the mound followed
by relatives and friends of the departed, each given a rose
with which to decorate the mound.

I look around for what seems like the first time and,
in trying to extricate myself from the moment, I count up
to seven other similar gatherings. I'm sure there are more

such assemblages beyond my eye's reach, behind the trees. I wonder what sorts of stories attach themselves to those individual assemblies – I wish those trees could talk! Is there someone in shoes akin to mine? Only they would truly empathise with me and understand my decision not to attend the three-day mourning at Umaga's and the funeral service at church earlier today.

What I don't understand is why I yielded to Musa and Michelo to come here and be the subject of every pulsating tongue, the specimen under the microscope of every pair of eyes. 'I'll drive you there bro, join us!' Musa had said, sounding more authoritative by the word. His wife had added, 'We've already missed church, trying to convince you to at least attend the burial. Yes, people will talk but trust me, whatever happens today, this will give you some release... closure. Please come with us.' They had said it was only to say bye; that it would be unheard of if I shunned her burial. Now and here, I can read every unkind and unfounded thought racing in these many heads of different shapes and sizes and manifesting in their grimaces, frowns, whispers, harrumphing, stolen looks, and a general vibe of pushback in my direction.

Yesterday after wiping the house of every inch of her memory, I thought it was a cinch and the wound had formed a scab; that I would remember Mendy – if ever I did – only for the angel she was, not the devil she turned out to be. That was all. Not so today.

Today I feel as old and beat-up as the lorry that brought the Soweto boys to this place. It stands there, ready to break down any minute, and no *compos mentis* person would blame it if it did, for it has evidently seen many better days. It looks ancient. I feel for it. They use it without asking how it's doing, or if it still wants to be of service. Its windscreen is gone, its tyres smooth and cracked, its body black and rusty, face contorted and puckered, mouth slightly open (does it want to say something?); but it seems to possess a patient, understanding soul. It gives no thought to what others think and say about it; it continues to give of itself to these thoughtless humans – maybe it was made for that very purpose, to serve and question not, to die on duty trying to please humans who have the power to dump it for another whenever they are sure it has outlived its purpose. They ignore its wounds and attend only to its fractures; and even so, not because they care but because they want to use it even more. It is resigned to its fate.

Umaga, from between two slim, wet-faced women who appear to be making a great effort to look bereaved, stares at me unblinkingly. I think she knows every thought that has experienced life in my head. Those bloodshot eyes remind me of the Black-shouldered Kite. Then, half-recalled reports come in pounding gushes: 'Too much pressure on Mendy...her mother's fault. She says you're dry...a dead tree. She wants a grandchild...her only child. She thinks you're the one with a problem. Mendy loves you...' In all of this I never dreamed in aeons that Mendy would smash my heart so, much less with a friend – a very good friend until this, and he is dying.

Suddenly, all heads bow, including Umaga's and Musa's. The mouth prays, 'Dear Lord, help us to love one another, to pray for one another. In your name I paralyse the spirit of judgment among us; I cripple it!

'Let Sister Wendy's good works follow her. Indeed, she is dead to us but alive to you – because you are with her in paradise right now, where she will be forever. Therefore Lord, teach us to weep for ourselves, knowing that our sister is better off now. And help us draw inspiration from her many works: contributions to orphanages, to street kids, to her family, and last but not least to the furtherance of your gospel.

'In a special way, through the power of the Holy Spirit, comfort us all; but more especially her husband and her mother, whose tears will never dry and whose lives have forever been changed. Please Lord, let not the change kill them; let them learn to accept that death is the narrow road that all of us are destined to walk at the end of our journey on this planet.

'Dear Lord, please…' Then finally, the collective 'Amen!' And before anyone has time to say hi and bye, heaven's water breaks: drizzles, showers, and then tall rains. Everybody scampers: the majority into public buses (Hiaces, Coasters, and Rosas) and the lorry, the minority – like Musa, Michelo and me – into ordinary private cars. Umaga and her driver – flanked by the two slim women – walk imperiously to her latest Mercedes-Benz saloon, the prophet and his wife advance arrogantly on their red Hummer. Similar dispersals attend the other gatherings bar two, where they open umbrellas – I wonder what they're burying.

VI

I'm between the blue sky above and dark clouds below. The sky is bright despite the lack of sun, and the clouds appear to be rising as if to engulf me. I try to fly towards the blue but I haven't wings, and then I realise that I'm utterly naked. I cover my nakedness with my hands. A sinking sensation begins to rage in my stomach. I'm falling, and falling fast. Then two strong, invisible hands still me by my shoulders. The darkness below is unmoving. I'm not sinking. It's now the blue that's coming at me. I am rising, and, out of the blue, a sonorous voice booms, 'Behold your bride!'

All is calm and in its place. I look around but see no one.

'Do not look around and above. Look below!' the voice orders.

And, indeed, something begins to brighten the darkness, an ever-growing luminosity from below, it dazzles me, the brightest bright I have ever seen – like the sun. I raise one hand to cover my face. A sweet, familiar voice says, 'Honey, what would you consider unreasonable?'

I drop my hand. A luminous figure, whose physical features hide in light, floats in front of me, within touching distance. I want to speak, but my mouth refuses to open. The illumination begins to fade and I can see her piercing brown eyes. Then she becomes fully visible in her white gown.

I want to touch her face. I want us to go above the blue and never return to that place below the dark. I start to float towards her. Her gown turns black, her eyes like charcoal, she opens her mouth wide in time for me to see her incisors elongate and drip with blood, she raises her hands and her fingernails lengthen. I watch the transfiguration in terror.

The voice says, 'Kill him!'

And with one deft motion, she sinks her teeth into my neck and repeatedly guts my stomach with her nails. I feel the pain; I gasp for breath.

I start out of sleep in a cold sweat, breathless, chest heaving, panting. It's still dark. The digital clock on the side table registers 03:03 as I crawl out of bed and make for the small fridge near the door. I swallow a glass of cold water, and I'm back in bed in no time. Sleep eludes me and I sit up, in the dark, asking myself why such a nightmare. A week on after the burial and I thought I was doing just fine. Is it because Musa and I are visiting Vernon this morning? Or is it that, somehow, I must have dwelt on the thought of him and her together? Whatever the case, I have resolved to live my life: like that lorry, to harness a soul that is impervious to pain and shame, and like that bird to live safely in prickly conditions.

I catch myself trying to form Martha's appearance in my head – a chic and svelte lady, the chocolate version of Mendy. I recognise I have not met or spoken with her since three or four days before I received the call. And I'm here, picturing myself with her. I have never thought of her this way before. And odd as my corner of the world lately is, the thought and prospect of seeing her this morning warm my heart. Maybe it's because she's the only one I know who truly understands my pain and shame (and she doesn't need to tell me this – I know she does because I understand hers; she and I are in this together).

I get into the shower at 05:10 to be in time for the morning visiting hour from 06:30 to 07:30. And it's only a twenty-minute drive from my place to UTH.

VII

'He sustained extensive brain…tissue damage, particularly in the frontal lobe, and they say he's…obviously paralysed waist-down. You know…I'm not allowed to work his case,' Martha says, as her eyes begin to swim under a layer of tears.

'Yes. Yes, I know.' Pity starts to well in my heart. She's done nothing to deserve this. No one should go through this. She could have easily pulled out those tubes, ended the bastard's life and gone about a life of her own choosing; but she's here, being the good wife she's always been. And it's heart-wrenching that there's already all manner of scurrilous talk behind her back at the institution.

'They say, considering the extent of his injuries, anybody else would have probably died on the spot,' she says, as she swallows hard. 'Nobody understands how he's still alive.' She pulls a hankie from her handbag, dabs at her eyes, then brings it to her nose and blows into it. She's visibly exhausted and the dark semi-circles under her now reddened eyes tell her lack of sleep.

'Does anybody help you keep watch?'

'Yes. Lindiwe, his elder sister from the Copperbelt, and his mother. You know Lindiwe?'

'Well, I've only heard of her.'

'Yeah, that Lindiwe. Either she or her mother will come in around the end of this hour. I watch nights.'

The ICU feels smaller by the minute. Light rain starts to fall outside, and Musa is not yet here. I wonder what's keeping him. But, there's a part of me that doesn't want him to come today. It's all so bizarre that in this melancholy there's a contradiction, largely restrained by the thudding heart of the heavily bandaged body between us, whose only visible features are closed eyes (and I hope they never open), nostrils with a colourless tube in each, and broken lips forced to remain slightly open by another tube. There are other tubes, connected to machines, creeping under the blue sheet that hides him from the world. I want to ask about the tubes, but I choose not to. I have a rough idea of what purpose they serve. Besides, it's better to let her say only what she wants.

'Peter, I really don't know how to feel about all this. Oh my God!' Tears freely trickle down her cheeks as she breaks into a sob. 'You're...you're the-the only person who-who-who can under-ssss-tand my...'

'No. Oh, no. Please don't. Um, just take it easy. It'll be fine. You'll see.'

I don't remember covering the distance between us, but she's in my arms, her head on my chest, her arms tight around my back. My hands should stay high, on her shoulders, yet they slide down slowly and press into the small of her back. Her torso pushes into me. She gasps and exhales. Our bodies have never been this close before. I take in her sweet feminine scent. But her body rocks and jolts in my embrace, so I continue to tell her it'll all be just fine, just fine, just fine. In truth, I don't even know the meaning of what I'm saying. How on earth will it all be just fine?

Love Letters

Set me as a seal upon thine heart, as a seal upon thine arm: for love
is strong as death; jealousy is cruel as the grave: the coals thereof
are coals of fire, which hath a most vehement flame.
Song of Solomon 8:6

The instrumental of 'Here Comes the Bride' is a form of an agonising slow death – the sort you would wish on a convicted serial killer. The ceiling fans give the slow death more reach, and every waft of air is a near-successful attempt at asphyxiating me. Granted, this experience is proving increasingly enervating and against logic, but I can't give up today; I have to see this through – no matter what.

Mulezu, my childhood friend and former college-mate, and I are two of the wedding guests seated in the gallery. Below, I can see in the middle section, next row from the flower-festooned elevated pulpit, a familiar grizzled head next to another familiar head wrapped in a cream-white headcloth. Next to them are unfamiliar heads. From our vantage point the heads and their movements play out like a film, and the pulpit is the perfect stage.

When people turn to face the entrance where the bride is to be escorted in, I wonder who's doing the handover because the grizzled head obviously isn't. I've never seen this before, even Mulezu agrees it's eccentric. The music mixes with the excitement of the chattering guests. The church is near full. Then the grizzled head's little brother, who seems to be gliding on the parquet floor, makes an entry arm-in-arm with the bride, whose face sits seemingly peaceful under a white gossamer veil, her eyes glued to her bouquet of white lilies, her radiant form floating in time with the tune. He'll hand her over to the groom midway between entrance and pulpit. But, why is the bride's uncle doing the handover?

The pastor stands in anticipation in the pulpit. Before I know it, the impeccably dressed groom and his father, a famous Lusaka businessman, materialise from I don't know where and he is now arm-in-arm with her; and the DJ, in a glass-walled control room near our pew, changes the music to Scott Wesley Brown's 'This is the Day.' There's ululation in the air. The two heads are stationary; their faces focus on the pulpit where the bride and groom are ascending the three steps to reach their royal-looking chairs draped in white cloth, with yellow lilies attached to their sides. The groom, in the most gentlemanly manner, leads the bride to her seat before he takes his. It's all so beautiful to behold. Perfection.

Mulezu and I sit here repeatedly eyeing each other and wondering whether we have any right to attend this service. I want to leave, but something in me says I'm in the right place at the right time. So, I sit and wait, as I soak in all the feeling of the wedding. I imagine that I'm the groom. How resplendently glorious it would be!

Mulezu gives me a nudge and says, 'I know you'll not turn back now, but are you sure of this?'

I'm long in answering, but just in time my thought becomes words, 'Yes, I am.'

II

Cholwe and I were only fourteen and fifteen, respectively, when we fell in love. Our love began at the beginning of Grade Eight, just before I went to Luangwa. And because we didn't have handsets in those days, we didn't own anything smart to give us among other apps WhatsApp, Facebook, Instagram, and Snapchat. So, we wrote letters – love letters. We felt alive; it was as if our hearts had just started beating, and our blood started coursing sweetly in our veins – and everything was beautiful. Our lives had just begun. She said our love was, in essence, the beginning of the stars; I said our love gave the stars license to shine. We were birds of a feather from the beginning (you should have seen us; Cupid had struck our hearts).

With her, Walter Trobisch's book title 'I Loved a Girl' made so much sense in the present tense, and I gave her Deborah Kent's novel 'Te Amo Means I Love You.' She came with an influence that said my chemical heart was in love, met my unfettered heart with her unbridled heart, and we knew we would forever be inseparable. Young as we were, we found there would never be anything as powerful and insuperable as two young hearts in love.

Cholwe and I always felt connected; and when she went to Kamwala Secondary and I went about 400 kilometres away to Luangwa Boarding, dreams became ever more soothing, and days presented as cheery entities in the stream of time.

I had a special photo I would gaze at every night in bed. In it, she stood against the roughcast wall of her family house, unshod and in a pink dress that was a canvas of white lilies, her tawny beige skin almost gold in the sun, and her not-so-black, close-cropped hair stood proudly on a head that carried an ever-smiling sylphine face. It was as though everything bright, noble and happy lived inside the small photo I'd hold in my palm. She had an air of ease and constancy about her, and she was insensible to any of the mockery I suffered at the hands of my seniors. She stood there, night after night, smiling, exuding something that suffused me with the strength to face each day.

Then I received a letter from her. I'd open and reread it next to her smiling self every prep night just before studying. This went on for the whole of the final month of the first school term. It was as if she were there with me, especially when I'd hear a love song play that was one of the end-of-letter dedications. And so, our love grew stronger with every day spent apart.

My stint at Luangwa didn't last more than a term. I couldn't go back there owing to my parents' poverty. In truth, they couldn't send me to any school. So, dad checked his archives and retrieved his father's cousin who lived in Kafue, fifty kilometres south of Lusaka. I remember him telling me, 'You can see for yourself how poor we are. It's because of this that you're not going back to Luangwa, and it's also the reason why you have to go and live with your grandpa in Kafue. I've never met him, but I hear he lives on a farm. He'll send you to school there. This is the only way to continue with your education, and I'm sure you'll be well taken care of.'

My time in Kafue was interspersed with Cholwe's letters and visits. Our love took on a new dimension, more meaningful. And more than visualise our future together, we felt it. It was then that I started trying to talk her into performing an oath thanks to the influence of a romantic African film I'd just watched, whose name I forget. A young man and woman were so madly in love they decided to perform an oath. The couple half-filled a small calabash with water, then made cuts in each other's right thumb deep enough to bleed. They then pressed and rubbed their bleeding thumbs together over the water; the mixed blood started to drip into the calabash and after several drips, they French-kissed, swirled the liquid in the calabash to dye the water red, and then drank it. When the calabash was empty, they broke it into a myriad shards and hurled it into the river on whose bank they stood declaring, 'Our love will not end until a blind soul puts our calabash back together. Our love is forever.' They looked at each other, smiled and kissed some more. Their sunset act, though bizarre, somehow appealed to my wild heart.

I know it sounds weird, but she and I'd sit under the Kafue Railway Bridge on the concrete slab a few metres from the crocodile-infested Kafue River and I'd think, Why not? I'm here, she's here, the river is here, and we love each other. Besides, finding a calabash would be a cinch. And I was even more encouraged when I convinced myself that we loved each other even more than the couple in the film.

We would make many promises to each other, but I wanted more – the oath. She'd say, 'I'm not doing anything that crazy! You're my one and only, and forever you will be. If you don't believe me, just wait for I know time will tell. Yes, time will tell.' She'd look a little deflated, after which I'd say, 'Sorry. I believe you. Forget the oath.' But, that was only before bringing it up when next we'd meet – maybe it was the kissing I really wanted. It took some time before the hold of the film would fade on me and eventually leave our relationship alone.

III

Today is one of those days when I need not only to have, but also to express the courage of my convictions or the situation will be too marred to salvage.

After the hymn 'Love at Home,' the over-confident groom (who's just about my age, except famous and rich because his father – in attendance with his wife – is famous and rich) takes the microphone and owns the pulpit. He stands tall and athletic, clad in one of those princely, black, tailor-made Italian suits, a white shirt so white I'm sure I've never donned anything like it, and a smile that illuminates his chiselled face. He starts to talk about poets, philosophers, gurus, teachers, and sages having tried throughout the ages to define love but to no avail. He sounds polished, alluring; his school years away in Britain have served him well, for he oozes an air that's definitely far above my class – as at now. He says the world is not any closer to a definition of love we all can subscribe to. He says love is a mystery. I agree. He then starts talking about some of the craziest things children say about love and marriage, and there's laughter. I catch myself smiling, even Mulezu can't help it.

Without warning, the groom breaks into a rendition of Newsong and Natalie Grant's 'When God Made You.' He sings his heart out to the bride, and it's clear his voice is all the instrumentation he needs. So sweet. The atmosphere fills with Amens and wows. Either he's genuinely in love or he's just plain stupid because he knows her heart is elsewhere. In fact, the two heads also know it.

Fast-forward: The pastor concludes his sermon on marriage. Susan Ashton's 'Love Will Be Our Home' starts to play. He motions to the bride and groom to stand. He waves a hand; the song stops. He says, 'We've been moving towards the top of the mountain. I can tell you now that we are almost there. Therefore, if there's anyone in this congregation with any just cause why these two must not be joined together in holy matrimony, please say so now or forever hold your peace.' He looks around and waits awhile. 'If you have any good reason why these two must not be joined together in holy matrimony, please speak out now or forever hold your peace.' He waits another moment. 'Okay, it is well. Let's proceed.'

The bride and groom stand about a metre apart, with the pastor almost between them. He produces a small notebook, opens it, and moves the microphone closer to his mouth. I must be seeing things, but the bride seems a little aquiver in my eyes. She's fidgety, as the vow resounds. I imagine the struggle and sorrow veiled by the white, and I know, in this moment, it's my fault. I've failed her.

The groom says, 'I do.'

IV

There was this one time when we crossed the bridge and followed the railway in the direction of Mazabuka and detoured from it to enjoy some shade under a fig tree. I'd written her a letter to which she'd replied before the visit; we were taking our relationship to the kissing level.

As we'd talked under the bridge in our usual spot that day, things didn't feel the same, there was something inviting and forbidding in the air between us. I'd thought about how the sun kissed the river so freely, how the earth embraced creation, how the rains hugged the earth, how bees kissed flowers, and wondered what all these mellifluous nuances of nature were worth if she didn't kiss me. So, unwilling to continue with the awkwardness, I suggested we saunter down the rail. And now here we were in the shade, the grass and birds singing, episodes of cool air enfolding us, we looked at each other and had nothing to say.

It was normal for me to have nothing to say, but it wasn't for her. She was the type who always had something to talk about, from school, to family, to church, to friends, to future – and more. Her silence coupled with the way she now stole looks at me was unusual.

The awkwardness continued.

I mumbled something about the letter. She nodded. Then, at a speed to rival lightning, we were locked, tongue on tongue; it was an awkward connection, salty, dry. We didn't know how to execute it. We disconnected in a heartbeat.

The kiss was a brutal awakening. But in its brutality lay something gentle, sweet, uniting. In my heart, it was all the oath I needed. Also, for the first time, my testes hurt – it was like nothing I'd ever felt, and she wasn't to know.

As we walked back on the railway line, arm-in-arm, laughing, a shabbily-dressed, visibly malnourished old man – most likely septuagenarian – on a bike riding towards the bridge saw us and shook his head in disapproval. He made as though to say something, then locked his mouth. In our world, we didn't care what a prejudiced old man, or anyone for that matter, thought about us. We were disciplined enough not to have sex before wedlock, at least according to a promise we'd made to each other.

As we sauntered back to the bridge, for some reason, the sun didn't feel as sweltering as before the chapter in the shade. We joked, laughed, and I kicked stones. When finally under the bridge again, there was only invitation in the air between us. That awkward moment was gone. We were recreated. We knew we would always love each other.

I pulled a piece of paper from my back pocket. It carried two verses of poetry I'd written for her the day before. I read it to her to the chorus of rippling water and singing grass, as she sat in a pose that reminded me of the Buddha, her full lips and eyes closed, and her head ever so slightly tilted back.

> You are to me a blessing,
> Like every new morning.
> It's you I'll always love,
> No soul this love can move.
> Many hope to see us fail,
> But this love is indeed a pearl;
> It turned me into a poet.
> These are words from the heart.
>
> Made to choose from the start,
> You would still be my onliest.
> Being with you is heaven,
> Where I wish to be taken.
> Such an angelic love is paradise,
> It is indeed our first prize.
> I stand in love complete.
> These are words from the heart.

She transformed right before my eyes. She came alight with every line. I became convinced she was the brightest of all diamonds, and my love was the sun that made her shine. We were destined for each other.

V

'Do you, Cholwe Milimo, take this man…?' The rest is out of focus.

Through my blurred vision I see the bridesmaid steadying the bride. The pastor pauses, leans in, and appears to be conferring with the bride, while the groom's face begins to lose its hold and melt into something unrecognisable, an attendance of chagrin or fear.

I more sense than hear the low murmuring rumble ripple through the church, and all the while Mulezu is urging, 'Now. Do it now!' He must have said it a little louder than intended because heads turn towards us in the gallery. The man seated three people to my right looks a bit too quizzically at us. He looks surprised and angry all at once. I bounce back his look but he doesn't budge. I'm afraid he's going to say something. What the heck! I stand up, the man makes as if to stand also, but he stays put and his face registers surprise. He shifts his eyes to the pulpit.

Something encouraging pumps my veins. Then I remember having reread all her letters yesterday, from the very first one about the beginning of the stars to the very last one about our eternal love sealed with a kiss and witnessed by the fig tree, and how I vowed to myself to give them an enduring meaning. It's now or never.

VI

Most of those who knew us said we'd begun to resemble each other, whereas some suggested we might have been siblings in past lives – whatever that meant! Anyway, we never took them seriously until one day at the bridge when a guy, who looked a little older than me, called me to the side and asked me to put in a good word for him with my sister. I refused to be offended – actually, I liked it. I went back to him and said she'd said no, after which he looked disappointed and walked away. We laughed hard (I don't know why exactly, but it was funny). He made us feel a tad stroppy, but we came around and would even sometimes introduce ourselves as siblings just for effect.

I would, on every one of those special nights in bed, reminisce about each minute we'd spent together at the bridge. I'd try to remember everything she'd said, and I'd see her in my mind, as if she were right there with me. I would almost feel her warm breath on my neck. I'd fall asleep, and then we were together at the bridge, watching the river, her lips sometimes opening, closing, and opening again, shaping the words: 'Everything I write to you is true. I mean it. Our love is forever. I love you and always will. Please, read the letters again.'

VII

I summon my voice and let it out in dimensions to fill the building, 'I have something to say!' I sense the tremor in my voice, but it's intelligible. All heads turn to me and I feel eyes all over me; some of these heads must be wondering what manner of madness has befallen me. I'm focused on the pastor but somehow I see everyone, even those seated behind me. The bride removes the veil and looks up at me. I know she was starting to believe I wasn't here. She must have thought I'd become chicken-hearted, a coward. Life starts to replace the lifelessness on her face; she holds her peace. The groom's face recedes further from the sublime to the ridiculous to the tragic. The two heads, now facing me, are images of the most bewildered demons.

There's silence, peace almost.

The pastor looks nonplussed. He seems to be playing chess in his head or engaged in life-and-death computations. In fact, he's immobile. 'I have something to say!' I repeat clearly. Then his head moves. His eyes sweep across the assembly as though to ask permission on my behalf. He tilts his head downwards; his shaven chin touches his grey tie. I continue, 'These two would be unequally matched if they were to be joined in holy matrimony. The reason is simple: she loves another and her parents and the groom know that! I can tell that the groom is sincere in his love, but she'll never learn to love him or anyone else for that matter. I'm sorry to be the one to spoil this beautiful party. But, what can one do when all else fails?' The eyes burrow into me. There's now an undercurrent of muffled voices, yet all the mouths appear to be closed. I see on the faces varying shades of intense interest, wonderment, worry, fear, resignation, and other things unknown to me. And my imagination of the two bewildered demons is becoming odder by the second. Maybe – just maybe – they'll learn that love exists in the space beyond tribe and privilege; maybe they, and others here, will learn, too, not to awaken the unreasonable, almighty monster in the gentle thing called love.

The pastor composes himself and says, 'Can you please tell us, who is this person that she's so in love with?' He says it as a challenge.

'Me!' There's an ephemeral surge of voices, as I continue, 'Yes, she's in love with me. It's me she really wants to marry.'

The pastor moves the microphone to her face. 'Yes, I love only him. Sorry mum and dad, but you gave us no choice.'

The groom appears to be struggling to stay standing. His legs fail him, and he slumps down into his seat. The best man scurries to his side and begins to fan him with what appears to be a wedding invitation card, in utter discount of the ceiling fans.

I descend the staircase very quickly and approach the pulpit. Mouths open speechlessly and eyes threaten to leave their sockets. Something they see only in films has come upon them. The groom's parents appear indifferent and immune to the goings-on – it could be that the impulse hasn't reached their brains yet. The fanning continues over the now surprised eyes and the gaping mouth in which something pink slurps at the air. The pastor is again immobile; confusion on his face. The video recordist is the odd one out: he smiles widely, as he focuses and refocuses the lens of his machine.

Cholwe, face fully exposed and looking revitalised, shakes off her white stilettos, lifts the floor-sweeping dress from behind her and holds it by her right side a little above the knees. I grab her left hand; we dash for the exit. Mulezu trails us to his old model Toyota Corolla. We jump into the back seat and hug tightly, refusing to let go, lest we lose the moment. Her warm breath lingers on my neck. And, imagined or not, I hear Vince Gill's 'Look at Us.' Then, as swift and surreal as a dream, we cruise away to our future in the squeaky old car, while the rear-view mirrors reflect a growing gathering of dazed faces and flower-draped latest luxury cars – a receding picture of something begging to be forgotten.

Something Broken

In the confrontation between the stream and the rock, the stream
always wins - not through strength, but through persistence.
Buddha

A t a secret location in a bush of tall trees, thickets, and
tall grass, something is about to start. It's midnight and
the full moon looks on. The owls' hooting gives rhythm and
mood to the tense stares of two men who stand facing each
other on this cleared circular spot, which appears to have
known the weight of men for some time now. The men size
up each other as if they are meeting for the first time. They say
nothing. Wind howls and it feels cold.

Just like these two men appeared here one after the other,
a third man materialises from the grass. The two nod in his
direction. They seem to revere him. He clears his throat. They
remain standing, waiting. Two other men, almost at the same
time, walk into the circle from opposite directions. They nod
in the direction of the third man, and then to the others. The
third man brings his left wrist close to his eyes and dwells
on the watch, at which time a sixth man appears. All of them
are clad in black gumboots, bush-green overalls and matching
gloves.

The third man squats, the others follow suit. He clears
his throat, looks around, and a satisfied air possesses his
facial features. 'We are all here. It is good,' he says. 'My job
tonight is both simple and very important. We are moving
our mobilisation and operations to a level never before seen
in our country, but it is necessary. And we have not only the
material and technical support, but also the blessing of our
top leadership. We have friends from down south who are
experienced in the mechanics of our next operational phase.

I need to know that you all still have the same burning commitment to our cause; and if you feel like quitting, please leave now.'

There's a moment of silence in which the men steal looks at one another. More silence still.

'Okay. I take it we're all of one mind. In which case, I now need you to listen carefully – and please ask if something is not clear.'

What follows is a monologue spelling out strategy and targets. The other men listen intently. A discussion follows. All the men speak with such passion that the grass around them would smoulder and burn if it weren't fresh, as though to reaffirm to the third man that they were ready to die for the cause. The owls continue having a say, as the wind picks up and pummels against and through the grass, causing it to whistle monotonously, and the moon lends all its luminescence.

II

The weather is cold, thick dark clouds gather above him, creating a deep-grey blanket, and lightning punctuates the Lusaka sky. His wont of a walk is about to become a nightmare. He looks at his wristwatch. *This Friday stroll is not going well.*

Kumani has made it a habit – almost a ritual – to take excursions around his neighbourhood twice a week, usually between 3 and 6 p.m. It has become an outlet for the frustration, anger, and gloom that beset him. He extricates his being, mostly thinking about the meaning of freedom and its supposed bearing on politics, religion, and love. He has found himself thinking more about these things from when he was seventeen – two years ago.

He thinks about how this year – 1964 – in Northern Rhodesia is a blend of hope and despair: hope because of the spirit of the people that refuses to be broken, believing they will be free one day, and despair owing to the continued colonisation by the British, which feels, to locals, no different from suffocation. One can tell that expectation for independence is in the air against the backdrop of some British colonies having already gained theirs in this decade.

Being an avid listener to *BBC Radio*, like his father, he's aware that Kenya gained independence from the British two months ago, Ghana in 1957, Nigeria in 1960, Sierra Leone in 1961, and Uganda in 1962. He wonders why independence hasn't come to his own country yet. He feels his fists clench. Above he sees a drenched bird on a tree branch, immobile, without song, eyes fixed on the ground, enduring the storm; he thinks the sight is synonymous with black Northern Rhodesians. It gives him a measure of hope that the main political party in opposition to the colonial government is now vehemently saying that the activities of the *Mau-Mau* will seem like child's play if the British don't grant independence.

He starts to walk back home more urgently, to escape the nascent February rainstorm and the verbal avalanche and/ or physical punishment his father will likely unleash on him if he gets home late. He recalls a day, almost two years ago, when he got home after sunset: no sooner had he completed his sentence about a rainstorm having been so blinding that he had to take refuge and wait it out than his father slapped him senseless. Although he didn't feel himself fall to the living room floor, a ringing started in his ears, and a sharp pain streaked through his head like lightning, marked by his mother's alarmed voice, 'What have you done to him?' He heard his father say, 'Woman, go back to the kitchen!' But, that was then. Lately, he suspects that his father now sees him as a man and will probably never treat him like a boy again. But, he knows only a fool would fully trust their suspicions. He glances at his watch again. A smile breaks his chiselled look. Annoying his father isn't an option.

It's now pouring, lightning is relentless. He breaks into a jog. *Twap-lap, twap-lap, twap-lap* is the rhythm of his flip-flops: feet into puddles of muddy water at every *twap-* and mud plastering the backs of his brown knee-length shorts and black T-shirt at every *-lap*, as he increases his speed. The ominously cold rain causes his skin to cringe, and his toes, fingers, ears, and nose-tip begin to bite. There is, at the same time, a warmth building from within, spurred by his physical activity.

He remembers a time in his village when he was fifteen, a year before his father made the decision to relocate the family to Lusaka in search of a better life; he was, with his friends Omili and Linoku, on a chase of a wild pig that had, somehow, managed to free itself from their trap when they were about fifty metres from it. What was supposed to be an easy kill morphed into a dangerous chase through the bushes and thickets of the Amogawi forest, witnessed by a rainstorm as frigid and fierce as this.

It crosses his mind several times to remove his flip-flops to run better, but there's no time to stop. The rain is torrential, and visibility is becoming limited to about twenty metres. He sees several people hurrying in different directions in a desperate attempt to escape this now interminable storm. A heavyset woman crossing the road slips and falls into muddy water a few metres in front of him, a man in bush-green overalls with an ugly scar on the left side of his face runs past her, she stands up, looks around, fishes her *chitenge* from the water and quickly wraps it around her waist, in time to resume her escape.

Isn't it just amazing how nothing on earth gets people busy and running like rain, especially when it joins forces with lightning and its noisy evidence?

His watch has stopped and it's staring at him. He almost blames himself for it but quickly realises that there's no securing it in this rain. His blood now courses warmly through him, his heart beats riotously, his breathing is a dog's gasp; he can feel his toes, fingers, ears, and nose-tip begin to warm up. He's totally wet, but the water that now soaks him feels pleasant – he has become a heater.

Kumani now sees the red brick house – their rented family house – and knows he's only a minute or two away. Darkness is fast embracing his neighbourhood, a poor residential area on the western periphery of Lusaka, a burgeoning city since 1935 when it became the new capital of Northern Rhodesia.

The lamp casts his father's energetic shadow on the living room curtain.

Mr Mbasa usually gets home by sunset after leaving the Smith's house. He works as a houseboy for the Smiths, three years and counting, his first and only job since leaving the village. The crop of the 1959-60 farming season failed, prompting him to contemplate moving his family to Lusaka in the light of stories of migrant labourers making a living of sorts in Lusaka or on the Copperbelt, especially the latter.

Lusaka mostly offers employment to Africans in domestic and construction works, while the Copperbelt province is an economic kernel boasting huge investments in copper mining by, among others, Bwana Mkubwa, Roan Antelope, Anglo-American Corporation, and Nchanga Mine.

Mr Mbasa had already started accepting the idea of going to look for work on the mines when his church friend, Mr Malowe, who worked – and still does – as a clerk in Mr Smith's office, informed him that his boss was looking to employ a married and responsible middle-aged Christian man as houseboy.

Kumani's run comes to a halt at the doorstep, breath in laboured gasps. The house has an awning of extended asbestos over the kitchen door area. He's now under this umbrella. Water trickles down from his short hair to his thick eyebrows; some of it ends up in his big eyes. He opens his mouth wide, revealing a set of near-white teeth, inhales deeply through his nostrils, and exhales through his mouth. He repeats this two more times; it's his way of reverting quickly to normal breathing. His athletic, slender body always responds well to this.

He can see the sparkle of pools of water everywhere he looks in spite of the darkness. The soil is clay in this area, so floods quickly form every time it rains heavily. All the houses, without exclusion, are in disrepair in this slum.

An angry bolt of lightning rams across the sky, and an even angrier thunder follows; the sound is deafening, and the ground shifts a little. He knows better than to stay outside any longer. Four fatalities due to lightning have so far been reported since the beginning of the rainy season.

He knocks on the door.

'Who's there?' It's his sister's voice.

'Fema, it's me!' he says, sounding like he's under attack, his right hand already holding down the door handle, ready to storm in. 'Hey! Unlock the –.'

She unlocks the door before he can complete the sentence. 'You're all wet!' she observes, as if she expected him to come out of the rain dry. 'You must learn to read the clouds,' she says, her eyes transmitting something mystically warm that it can only have come from her heart. She has a way with language; she was a precocious child and grew up to seem always years ahead of herself in both diction and demeanour.

Kumani thinks Fema is too overbearing for a seventeen-year-old little sister. He knows she loves him dearly and is overly protective of him – after all he's her only brother, and she his only sister. Still, he does not like it when she reprimands him. In truth, he's sometimes more in awe of her scathing words than his mother's whenever there's cause for a rebuke.

He can now hear the crackle of the radio from the living room over the sound of rain and thunder. He knows his father is in there, waiting for his favourite 6 p.m. one-hour news on Africa – mainly on independence movements in sub-Saharan Africa. He's found himself getting increasingly drawn to the programme lately.

He and his father usually sit on their wooden benches, listen to reports from BBC correspondents and later talk about the state of sub-Saharan Africa as it pushes for independence. He remembers once hearing something about the British government urging the Colonial Office to exercise caution, saying a quick and careless transition of power to Africans, for the sake of it, wouldn't be good for the colonies and that a shift of power must take into consideration Africans' preparedness to govern themselves.

While his father couldn't agree more, Kumani thought it was merely cheap propaganda to justify British colonisation of much of Africa. His mind boggled at the idea that Africans didn't know governance, thinking of the cultural dignity of governance that suffused the African leadership system – chiefdoms, villages, councils, and the meticulous structures of rule and representation at every level.

Kumani thinks the kitchen's rather claustrophobic today. As he still feels the urge to breathe in deeply after his run, it could probably be because the doorway between the kitchen and the living room – as are all the others in the house – is hung with a heavy, dark-coloured curtain material. He ambles into the living room. He now breathes freely in the relatively spacious room, with its small wooden dining table and accompanying four wooden chairs in one corner, and two wooden benches that can sit three to four people each, situated in the centre. It's 6 p.m. and the programme is starting. His father is seated on one of the benches. He figures his mother must be in the bedroom.

'How are you my boy?' his father says, his big, fiery eyes inspecting him from head to toe, and back to head.

'I'm fine dad. How are you?' This he says with the traditional gesture of deference.

'Get yourself dry clothes!' It's an order.

There are three doorways from the living room, each leading to a bedroom; he takes one. He dons dry clothes hastily and darts back to the living room. He sits on the bench opposite his father, the radio between them. The heavy rain seems to make for a rather peaceful, warm atmosphere in the house. Palpably warm because of the two braziers his sister is using to cook supper in the kitchen. It's a small house that gets cold or warm quickly. The braziers spur the latter.

Kumani wants to shout out something to his sister, but he knows better than to make noise when the news is on. He stands up quickly and starts for the curtain. The smell of onion and *kapenta* greets his nostrils, his stomach churns with anticipation, and he knows how deeply hungry he is. He hears his mother's voice in the kitchen. He pulls the curtain aside and says, 'Mum, how are you?'

'I'm fine Kuma. How are you?'

'Fine.'

'Your sister was just telling me about how soaking wet and terribly muddy you came in…' It is more of a question than a report.

'Yeah, it was bad.' He almost turns back to the living room, forgetting what he has gone to the kitchen to do. Then he says, 'Fema, please heat bath water for me when you have a free brazier.'

'Okay. The relish is almost done. I'll heat your water, Kuma.'

It's almost thirty minutes into the news and there's no mention of Northern Rhodesia. He looks at his father, fascinated by how totally attentive he is, not only listening but also watching the radio in a way that is difficult to see if his eyes blink. The programme does not seem to captivate his ears and eyes only, but his entire being as well. Kumani's mind wanders momentarily, then he hears his father say, 'Listen…listen carefully!'

Finally, there's a story on Northern Rhodesia. It's about the *Cha-Cha-Cha* uprising. His father's face lights up, his unblinking eyes fixated on the radio as if to suck it in; his large, flat nose and wide mouth twitching slightly, his jaws locked, and deep lines cross his forehead from temple to temple. His well-trimmed moustache and hair don't seem to soften his appearance in this moment. Kumani thinks the radio would have backed away in trepidation if it were animate. Such is the power of the gaze that the one gazed at gets intimidated; the gaze oozes with power – the gaze of such a man would be celestial and worshipped if he were rich.

They learn that there have been sporadic attacks in Lusaka and on the Copperbelt; white-owned shops were targeted with petrol bombs, some shops broken into and stock stolen, some main roads and those leading to government buildings blocked with rocks and burning logs and tyres; that the probably UNIP-engineered riots of locals against the colonial government will likely spill into tomorrow. The colonial police are implored to get themselves on top of the situation in the two areas.

Of very serious concern is the burning to death of a British woman reported on the Copperbelt. News is that she was trying to navigate her way home when the log-and-tyre-burning youths stopped her car. On seeing a white person behind the wheel, one of the slap-happy rioters threw a burning tyre into the car while others prevented the woman from escaping by placing huge logs around the car. The car couldn't move and doors couldn't open. She burned with her car. Besides, she was the wife of one of the top British politicians in that place. Did the rioters know who the woman was before they killed her? The reporters say they obviously knew and did this to send a clear message to the Colonial Office that they were willing to both kill and die to achieve self-rule.

Kumani and his father look at each other like trapped animals. They both seem to want to say something but they don't, choosing instead to listen on for more information. Something like this has never happened before in Northern Rhodesia. It's clear that the fight for independence is threatening to mutate into a bloodbath.

III

He floats just above the grass and, with the weight of a dream, he feels himself descend into himself. It's dark all around, and then light half-fills him. He starts to cough. He's not sure if he's coughing up blood, but his spittle is red. Is it all from his mouth? He sees the spittle on the ground near his face. The smells of wet earth and tall elephant grass bring the realisation that he's lying prostrate. He pushes his palms against the ground to lift his weight but every bit of him is sore. He tries again and this time he gets himself to his knees. His face under the layer of mud feels heavy and deformed. His nostrils feel a little blocked; he blows and a mix of red earth and blood jets out. He feels one-eyed; he sweeps his right palm across his face, feels the several bleeding swells and his left eye has become an aching mound that refuses to open. He turns his head to reconnoitre his surroundings, but the pain that pierces the nape of his neck is like nothing he's ever endured before. A grimace further distorts his swollen face, and he nearly cries out. He touches his hair and his fingers slide through the mud. He realises he's muddy all over. He wiggles his toes and it's clear he's without his sandals.

He wills himself to stand. His legs ache and quiver under him. His awareness starts to recover, so he turns his whole body around to get a sense of where he is. The last bit of the sun's flame has disappeared behind a hill and darkness is on its way. He heads west. He has to get to the road fast; so, painstakingly and carefully, he hobbles through the tall grass that seems to have already made way for him. He follows the trace and is soon on the road. It's only now he feels his whole head pound like a thousand hornets are stinging their way out. He staggers and slips in the mud but somehow he's still on his feet. His every fibre wants to stop, but he braves the pain.

Like a hunting lion approaching its prey, taking care not to make a startling sound, he walks slowly; only his case is different, he's tense, his throat dry, afraid that he won't be able to explain his state when he gets home. He can hear his heartbeat, which hammers so hard as if to break his ribcage; the sound is too much for his ears. *What will I tell dad? Please dad don't be home when I get there.*

But, he knows his father is very much likely at home now. The few times he gets home late is when he stops over at Mr Malowe's house, opting to listen to his favourite radio programme there and engage in discussion with his friend afterwards.

The Malowes and the Mbasas have been getting along very well since Mr Mbasa first arrived with his family in the city. Mrs Malowe, a very garrulous and tall, wide-hipped woman, is very good friends with Kumani's mother. The two women hardly spend a day without visiting each other. Usually they are seen saying goodbye to each other only to stand by the roadside and talk for hours, laughing and smacking hands at intervals. Sometimes they seem thoughtful as they talk, their hands slid under their *chitenges* as though barricading their pubic areas.

Meke, Mr Malowe's nephew, is Kumani's best friend. He accompanies Kumani on walks on very rare occasions. He doesn't see any benefit in walking around through – in his own words – 'squalor and poverty' as it only serves to do to him the opposite of what Kumani says it does for him. The last time he came along was almost two months ago. Bar the walks, the two are inseparable. The only thing that unsettles Kumani is that his friend seems to have taken a liking to Fema. He doesn't know for sure, but it's in how the two now talk to each other (like they are very important to each other) and look at each other (like they shouldn't look but they want to); he thinks something is a little out of phase. Above all this, they are best of friends.

He wishes Meke had accompanied him. He's sure he wouldn't have ended up like this. An irritation building in his bronchials interrupts his wish; he covers his mouth and coughs painfully. Air rips itself violently from the air sacs and thrusts the irritation out. Though it's now semi-dark and more darkness is falling fast, he can see blood-streaked phlegm on his palm; and as though to confirm it, his ribcage hurts in turn. He spits. All he wants now is to get home and see about starting to mend his broken body, not to answer questions about what he doesn't remember happened to him. He can almost see his father's fierce eyes bearing down on him and his mouth demanding answers, while his mother and sister look on pitifully.

Honestly, what happened to him? He racks his brain to no avail. He remembers leaving home to get some air, walking that familiar winding route and was on his way back when it all blacks out. It's as if a chunk of his memory has been stolen, the chunk that knows what happened to him. It's clear he's been brutally beaten, anyone can see that. But, why, how, and with what was he beaten? Was he left for dead? Or, was it a warning?

IV

The wood pops and crackles in places, as red and orange wriggly tongues of fire lick the cold air, causing it to spread something fleetingly embraceable to the men around it, each seated comfortably on an *indaba* stool made of wood and goat skin. It's expressly frigid tonight and other villagers have already taken refuge in their homes, but this round-fire meeting outside Lunzuwa's house has life. It's the only house with any sort of illumination outside; a dark sheet, in the absence of moonlight, has wrapped itself around the other houses. As the tongues busy themselves in the circle, the exposed skins of the men beam like liquid copper.

Kumani's eyes bounce from Linoku to Omili, wondering if the question posed by Lunzuwa has baffled them too. And as he expects, their foreheads furrow. Nzowa looks like undisturbed water. It's not easy to read him for anything.

How could he ask that – isn't it obvious?

The two friends were assigned by the headman to train the three young men in the 'acceptable ways of a husband' as they are expected to take wives anytime now. So, the five are usually together of late.

Nzowa is a married man while Lunzuwa was until eight months ago when his wife died. He's rumoured to already be getting too friendly with Mama-Mbili, that chatty woman whose late husband has long waned in people's memories. If it's true, it's clearly a dandruff on the scalp of tradition as he's not expected to get close to a woman until after a full year when the soul of his wife finally rests.

Lunzuwa says, 'Eh, what do you think?' His right hand rubs his bearded chin.

Nzowa charges, 'Yes. You are men now, you should think like such. Tell us.'

Kumani responds, 'I think, like other African countries that have gained independence, we shall succeed, and, yes, I think independence will be good for us. Isn't it just obvious?'

Linoku and Omili nod in agreement.

Lunzuwa says, 'I see that the three of you agree. Yes, independence will be good for us in and of itself because – I believe – no one wants to be ruled by outsiders. But, do you really believe that our politicians will give us back our country, that all people will have equal rights and privileges unmindful of tribe?'

Nzowa follows up, 'Uhm, when this excited charge towards independence dies – let's say we gain independence – are we going to be equal or some of us will be more equal than others? Linoku and Omili, what do you say?'

Kumani keeps his mouth closed. Linoku and Omili eye each other and confusion takes the space between them.

Nzowa continues, 'Omili, let's start with you.'

'You should know that I'm not versed in matters of politics, but–'

'Me too!' Linoku says. 'I'm sure Kuma can tell us about politics and tribes. He's from the city after all. Remember, it was he who told us about the white woman.'

Lunzuwa and Nzowa give Linoku a piercing look.

Omili says, 'I think we shall all be united. I think we shall all share in the euphoria of independence even long after Independence Day. Honestly, I see no sense in the thought that there's even a small chance some tribes will be maligned by other tribes. We are Northern Rhodesians, we are one, and we shall always be.' He says this with an air of someone who's sure they have hit the target in the dark.

Lunzuwa ventures, 'Well, let's keep that thought. Linoku?'

'Okay. I...I...I think I agree with Omili. Yes, I agree with Omili.'

Nzowa says, 'Yes you agree, but what do you think?'

'Okay. I agree that we are all Northern Rhodesians. And Kuma told me our people will give this country another name; maybe after that we'll not be as united as we are now – maybe some tribes will be more equal than others. I don't know but we'll no longer be Northern Rhodesians nor will we be fighting for independence. Things can change. Maybe we'll continue fighting – but for something else. It could be some sort or forms of recognition. I mean...I don't know, I'm just saying. Maybe we'll not be as united fifty years after independence, but I guess it will largely depend on our people.'

Lunzuwa enquires, 'You mean our politicians?'

'Yes, exactly.'

Nzowa says, 'Wow! For someone who wasn't willing to make a contribution, you've said quite a good lot.' His right hand beats down his unkempt hair. 'It's important to think about politics and leadership. You may become leader of our country tomorrow, or your children may, and we want a leadership that will bond all our tribes and put us all at a level in the eyes of the law and in how we shall be treated.'

Lunzuwa says, 'Uhm, wonderful thoughts! Kuma, what

do you think?'

'Well, if I was resurrected years after independence and found our country fractured on tribal lines I would die again – of a heart attack.'

'Wow!' Nzowa says, as Lunzuwa fixes his eyes more steadily on Kumani.

Omili asks, 'Is that supposed to be good, Kuma?'

Linoku chips in, 'Obviously bad! A heart attack over things you are not in control of?'

'Such is my conviction that I mean what I say,' says Kumani. 'See, I attended rallies in Lusaka and even participated once in breaking into white-owned shops. You should have seen our politicians vibrating as they painted the soon-coming beauty of our country, infusing all listeners young and old with courage to face death on the altar of freedom. They say we shall be the most prosperous nation in the world, with mining and agriculture as the beating hearts of our economy. They say we shall not fight any more, nor shall we pay for education and healthcare and agricultural input, that we shall have enough and more to spare, and that we shall all be equal – one nation under one leader who will champion unity and equality.

'You should see our politicians! They go to jail for us, they bleed for us, they are more than willing to die for us, and they live lives of sacrifice so that we may be free. Now,' he says, sweeping a look across the four faces to verify he has their attention, 'do you think our leaders are so insane that tribe will have any power to cause them to forget all this and destroy their own legacies by taking from us the very freedom they will have won for us?'

Silence.

Cold air clings to their backs. Omili stokes the fire, then stands up to fetch more firewood but Lunzuwa stops him, saying tomorrow is another night.

Lunzuwa, after another moment of silence, says, 'I admire your passion, Kuma. And, interesting as our discussion is, I'm sure we all need to rest, huh? It's been a very long, long day. Besides, no one is planning on dying tonight, huh? So, let's continue tomorrow.'

Nzowa nods repeatedly, as the young men bid their teachers good night and leave.

V

Tonight the young men talk not about marriage, but about politics and how they envisage their country post-independence. Linoku and Omili talk of a seemingly bleak future, while Kumani talks of a bright one. Still, both sides of the argument agree that it is of the utmost dignity for the country to determine itself. The topic feels misplaced as usually they talk about girls, marriage, and marriage lessons, and, being good hunters, about their hunting sprees in the Amogawi forest.

It's tradition to get marriage-age men to share the same house and do collective chores during their two months' lessons and apprenticeship, in which time each is expected to identify and/or win the heart of a would-be wife if neither he nor the girl is betrothed at the time.

Omili's childhood betrothed went to the city five years ago and it's whispered in some quarters that she's never coming back as she has found a city boy, while others allege she's already married. No one really knows for sure what is happening with Chisomo, but everyone seems to agree it would be foolery for Omili to wait for her as even her parents have cut contact with the village. So, the three friends are in the same boat – well, not really. Linoku has his sights on Namatama and he can swear by his father's grave the feeling is reciprocal; Omili talks of a girl whose name he doesn't know yet – and you will think she's an angel when he describes her – from the neighbouring village of Chavula, while Kumani can't take his heart off Tusekile.

Well, the trouble is Tusekile is married – and she lives in Lusaka with her husband, the man whose face, Kumani believes, can set off an earthquake. He remembers that face so unsmiling. But wait, he saw it smile once; he knew immediately it was better off unsmiling. Because when it smiled, that ugly scar on the left side of it became more menacing, crawling boldly from the temple and fading into the bearded chin only to reappear briefly on the neck before disappearing under the collar, and those bulging, bloodshot eyes an image of hellfire. To keep it simple, Kumani doesn't understand how she ended up with that monster or how she endures him. And now he's expected to find a wife in a place far away from where his heart is, from the one who owns his heart. He remembers the warmth of her breath on his neck and their laughter during those few stolen moments. Of course, it was all before that fateful day of the beating, which was followed by a painful month of healing at the end of which his parents thought it wise to send him to the village to marry and settle awhile until, maybe, after independence. They feared he might have been mistaken for an informant, in which case he was lucky to still be alive. It was well known that all suspected informants always ended up dead one way or another.

Linoku casts Kumani an examining look. 'Omili, let's forget the politics. Our friend here needs to at least identify a girl at the dance-off next week. And there's a chance she may be taken by the time he identifies her. Girls are everywhere, but he refuses to pick. All the beautiful girls will be coming here – all of them! Or do you want an angel to come down from heaven?'

'Stop being funny! My heart will confirm it when my eyes see right. I know this.'

Omili says, 'You have to see right next week. You just have to. It has to be next week, right?'

'There're matters you can decide and those you just can't. For instance, I can't order my heart to fall in love next week just because you want to see that happen. It's something that has to happen naturally – and the heart works in mysterious ways. We shall have to wait and see. I know that fine girls are coming from across the chiefdom for the dance competition next week, but what if the one who's supposed to be my wife chooses to stay away?'

Omili says, 'Then you'll choose another one! I don't believe in this thing of something already being there waiting for you – I think it's nonsense. Whether it's waiting or not, whether it's there or not, my friend just find something and make it yours.'

Kumani, to Linoku's laughter, says, 'I think you should concentrate on finding that girl and getting her name next week. Oh, you should also find out if she's engaged – don't forget that!'

Kumani hasn't told them about Tusekile, the girl who's just as angelic as Omili's description of his nameless girl. He doesn't think he can. He's trying desperately to forget her and move on. His eyes become heavy, he half-hears his friends talk and laugh, as he drifts into that world where dreams become reality and reality dreams, where gravity loses its hold and everything floats without regard for borders and boundaries, where souls venture to draw energy – sometimes puzzles, answers, and horrors – for the next day. It's that familiar part of the forest again, the wind blows, a black bird falls from the sky, he runs to pick it up, it tries to fly away but its wings are broken, and he's about to reach it when it all ends. Strange. It's the same almost every other night and he has lost count of it. He comes back, hears snoring and drifts off again.

VI

The sun is halfway across the sky, its rays a welcome warmth. The sweet collision of drums and traditional dance songs is the dominant feature in the air, as masquerade dancers – a mix of males and females – compete in front of eight elderly judges representing the villages present. This year's competition is happening here as the competition was won last year by this village's dancers – a feat of great measure owing to the talent on display every year. It's always prestigious when a village hosts the famous contest that unites the chiefdom. It's equally a very good time to make friends with visitors from the other villages and, also, for those searching to find spouses.

The village hosts hundreds of spectators whose immense pleasure it is to witness the dancers try to outdo one another to the manifest excitement of the spectators and judges, but especially of the spectators as the judges seem to have an unwritten rule that tells them to suppress their amusement which inevitably peers out at interludes before they remember to keep poker faces. Their job must be hard: to pretend you are not excited nor taking sides just so you can do your job. It's okay, because like gas in a human their excitement finds an outlet – if just for a split second irrespective of barrier.

Omili is looking out for the girl, and Linoku is focused on the dances. Kumani finds he can't concentrate on the contest, his eyes wander all over the place. He must have taken it very seriously in his subconscious to find a girl today. He has that feeling: one that tells you something is about to happen. He'll not admit it but he knows it has to be today. Driven, he furtively withdraws from his friends and finds himself going the circle, burrowing through ululations and charged chattering, and noticing how captivated the spectators are. The dancers seem to have cast a spell over the crowd.

He stops abruptly. *It can't be. It's not possible. Am I seeing right?* He looks down, massages his eyes, and looks up again. *Even if it's only the profile I see, it can't be someone else – and it can't be her. But – God! – what is this? How come? What's she doing here? Is it even her? I've never seen such resemblance. God!*

As though she has been waiting for him, she breaks the spell and turns her face in his direction. Her eyes freeze. He knows she's just as thrown as he. He never could have dreamed their paths would cross – collide – again, not in a thousand years of dreaming.

God! Despite the new scar just above her right eyebrow, she's just as beautiful as the last time I kissed her. Has she finally given up on years of abuse regardless of her parents' insistence on her having to fight to keep the marriage? God, if you give her to me now, she'll be my virgin and I'll never let her go.

Their hearts beat in time with each other, validating the language of their eyes. It's just like the old days, except they are free to love each other in the open, to fear death no more. Drums fade. Songs die. People vanish. They are alone.

She says, 'I thought I would never see you again.'

He says, 'You are mine. Our hearts are forever.'

She agrees, 'Yes my love, I'm yours – and you are mine forever.'

That smile, the one that weakens him at the knees, flashes and their love has just grown wings.

VII

The moon throbs and shimmers and shines, the grass whistles dully, and the owls hoot to what is now a familiar sight. Perhaps they are witnessing the last of these clandestine meetings. The concern of before has given way to satisfaction on the faces of the men, but their atavistic passion for self-rule remains high.

The man the others call *Boss* declares, 'We've met here every month since late last year and I promised you victory. Well, tomorrow night is our independence; we shall witness that foreign flag come down and ours go up. All our efforts – sweat, blood, tears – have culminated in our independence. Viva new nation!'

'Viva!'

'Viva one nation!'

'Viva!'

'Viva one leader!'

'Viva!'

'Viva black power!'

'Viva!'

'Yes. I shall see to it that you are all rewarded handsomely for your contributions to the fight. You made Northern Rhodesia ungovernable and because of that, independence has come to us. Thank you for engaging our women, in this fight, in the manner you did. Such passion, such courage to bare all in protest is unprecedented! It's only three weeks since they took their nakedness to the airport and the new Governor saw them in that state and turned back his plane in shame to London. Such was the impact of their public nudity that coupled with our own violent resistance, independence is upon us.'

The men listen intently, nodding their heads continuously, to every word *Boss* utters.

'You galvanised the men, the women, the boys, and the girls – you deserve credit!' He lowers his tone and speaks slowly, 'They tried, convicted, and hanged four of our own for the burning of that white woman – and our hearts still mourn their deaths – but I'm glad to announce,' he raises his voice, as though possessed by something alien, 'that their blood, too, has won us this victory and they shall forever be heroes in our eyes!'

'Yes!'

'Gentlemen, welcome to a country where equality of tribes will prevail, a country where we shall run the economy and ensure that our people will always have jobs, a country where prosperity will abound and our people will engage in business and industry, a country where corruption will have no place, a country where our interests will come first – our country, our democracy, our motherland! Viva!'

'Viva!'

Silence.

The men's faces look somewhat similar under the cover

of night, except that to *Boss*'s immediate right is a face with an ugly scar on the left side, a scar that crawls boldly from the temple and fades into the bearded chin only to reappear briefly on the neck before it disappears under the collar of the overalls. The face makes a menacing attempt at a smile, the bloodshot eyes bulging.

Silent celebrations abound, and the men's renewed collective optimism for their new nation merges in the circle and rises with promise, through the warm kisses of the moon, to the sky. And – behold! – the whole country from province to province, district to district, household to household, person to person, rises in the spirit of a nation born.

The Chant

For what shall it profit a man, if he shall gain
the whole world, and lose his own soul?

Mark 8:36

'Coin, coin, coin, coin. *Nipempako koini.* I'm asking for a coin. Please help. *Nati nipempako koini.*' Then repeat. The sound fades, as a realisation numbs my sense of hearing. I stand still, looking at him, convinced death would be more dignified.

He sits cross-legged on the edge of the pavement, with open, upturned hands. The irony is that he looks the polar opposite of the Buddha. The overhead October sun pours its fury on him, making him look nothing like my memory of him – he was never this dark, never so dry, never at all so helpless. And even if I gave him the coin he is asking for, it wouldn't buy him back his dignity. And what's wrong with his eyes?

The sun scorches even more harshly as if it's trying to say something, and in turn my temperature boils inside my smart suit; my tie is a noose getting tighter.

My face pulls and relaxes, my eyes widen then squint, but what I see refuses to make sense. Then a woman bumps my right hand with her handbag, my cellphone falls, I pick it up; its screen protector has cracked in many places. The woman stops and looks at me blankly. I prepare to say, 'It's fine. It's okay. It happens. Actually, it already had a crack.' Instead, her mouth opens, 'Ntss!' What just happened? She wobbles away to the pedestrian crossing, muttering something that sounds unkind. She looks over her shoulder and all I see is spite.

Like a most brittle sound, the uncreative and monotonous

repetition of each word in the same order pierces my ears and it's louder than when I first heard it. I'm sure the blind beggar is convinced that his next coin will come from the presence in front of him: me. As such, he makes sure I hear his every word so I'll have no excuse to not drop a coin into one of his open hands. With desperation written on his face, you would think there was more to a coin than that it could buy a sweet or a gum, like his next heartbeat depended on it. More pedestrians pass between us; I count eighteen but not one of them gives a coin. I stop counting.

I refocus on him: rheumy eyes with no sign of life, stubby nose, dirty beard that shrouds a mouth, tainted teeth, furrowed brow, and skin that should not belong to the living. His locks are overgrown and tousled, like it's been years since a blade last touched them. The soles of his feet come close to black and they evoke in me an eerie conviction that coins could slot into those crusted cracks, at least halfway. The rest of him is torn T-shirt and shorts synonymous with very dirty rags. Pity wells up in my heart.

I know what it means to be a beggar, albeit a different sort of beggar, for I was there a decade and a half ago.

II

In Grade Eleven and staying with my bourgeois uncle and his young wife, I could really understand how little they valued education and family ties. My uncle was one of those few men who had pulled themselves up by their own bootstraps. In brief, according to him, he grew up in the village herding cattle and absconding from school, seeing no value in sitting and listening to a teacher rumble on about things that didn't seem to promise a good life. His parents did not even try to impress on him the value of education because they did not know it themselves, nor did their neighbours, nor their headman. So his way ended up being that of the village: hard work and sweat, for a mere subsistence.

When an unmarried uncle of his called him to Lusaka to help with his struggling auto parts business, he grabbed the opportunity. He turned out to be a very good apprentice, working very well with his hands and showing a rare knack for business, and in time he mastered the trade just as well as his uncle, who would now, from time to time, leave him in charge of the business while he went to Dar es Salaam for orders.

In the space of three years, the business had started to generate sufficient profit that his uncle decided it was wise to cut out the middleman and go straight to the source. So Dubai became his bi-monthly destination for nearly a year before his Toyota Surf collided fatally with a tipper truck somewhere near Chikankata on his way to Livingstone where he was going to survey the market for expansion.

From the dust of the events that followed – the deceased's elder sister (who was enduring a marriage in Chawama) wanting to take over the business, the deceased's parents in the village wanting the business to be sold and money so realised given to them, my father demanding a stake in the business, and some village elders openly threatening him with 'a very bad outcome' if he did not give them some money – my uncle escaped with the business. This did not stop most of the village folk believing that he'd had a hand in the death of his uncle, allegations he always dismissed with, 'I worked hard to build this business. My uncle used to admit that I was to his business like sun and rain to a buried seed. I invested my sweat in it, and I am the only one with any right to this business.' Not a dismissal at all, but he saw it as such.

In time, just as it had been for his uncle, Dubai became his destination and he moved the business from Soweto to a much bigger shop on Chachacha Road.

Next, my thirty-year-old uncle married a town girl of twenty. Then a year into their marriage, family agreed that I join him because I was 'different,' in that I liked school and was very good at learning, and that Lusaka would be better for me and, if by chance I turned out needing to go to university, his money would guarantee my access.

When I first arrived at his house in Woodlands, I was convinced the president lived like him: two live-in maids, two gardeners, a cook, and security guards by day and by night. My uncle's wife, acting very friendly, ushered me into what would become my bedroom, the room that gave me the sensation of a soothing embrace. But outside the house it felt weird and almost claustrophobic: the remotely-controlled black gate looked formidable in its place and the four boundary walls rose high and carried atop a network of electric wires, and for the first time I felt imprisoned. As days came and went, I gradually got used to the comforts and luxury at my disposal.

My uncle took me to Kabulonga Boys Secondary and I enrolled in Grade Ten. It was easy because of my good Grade Nine results: I obtained the highest marks of any pupil in my district, a record in my village.

Fast-forward: things in Woodlands began to take on an alien form. My uncle and his wife looked less and less happy each day. Grade Eleven came and they hit a 'new normal': they didn't at all try to act happy for anyone, something between them was clearly breaking if not yet broken. Sometimes I could hear them argue in their bedroom. It all took a toll on my aunt, who looked parched more and more.

My aunt was one of those lovely, innocent-looking women – the sort to be cosseted. But her new reality was not in keeping with the angel that lay under the cracks. She was, after all, the one who stood up to my uncle whenever he'd return home angry and have a go at me with his insults and harsh words: 'Did they ask me, huh? Did they ask me if I wanted you here? Idiot! You will go to school but you will never reach my level. What did you bring, huh? What did those useless people in the village give you to come and "plant" here? One of these days I will send you back to the village.' And, 'Why are you looking at me like that? I am not your father! And when I finally chase you from here, I promise you, I will not want to see your face again.'

During the August school holidays, what little sparkle was left in my aunt's eyes vanished. Uncle became worse and worse, and soon there was one maid, who came at sunrise and left at sunset, one gardener, no cook, and no guard. The heavy black gate gave up responding to the remote control, and I ended up having to push it every morning and evening when my uncle left and returned. Then we stopped frequenting shopping malls and weekend cinema.

One day, as we sat on the sofa, my aunt said she had something to tell me. She slouched forward, her eyes focused on the floor. 'Look, I have to tell you this – I think you need to know. Your uncle's business is failing. He...' she paused, '... he suspects that people in the village sent you to bring bad luck here.'

'I-I-I don't understand. I have repeatedly told my uncle that I am here only for school, that's all. I don't have a-a-any reason to want to-to hurt him – or you.'

'I know. I know. He thinks they put "bad air" on you, of course without your knowledge. I don't know how long I can keep fighting for you to stay here; he really wants you out. I hope nothing goes wrong for him in Dar es Salaam.'

'Not Dubai?'

'No. Dar es Salaam. He's trying to go back to the basics and rebuild.'

'Oh, I didn't know it was that bad.'

'It is that bad.' She raised her head and looked me square in the eye. 'Considering that I've been fighting for you, do you think you can fight for me?'

'Yes. Yes, I can,' I said, convinced I could level a few mountains for her, for someone who was genuinely interested in my wellbeing.

Without breaking eye contact, she slid from her end of the sofa so that she could be right next to me. When her left hand rested on my right thigh, my heart palpitated wildly, my chest heaved. For the first time I saw something in her eyes that was drawing me in, something dark. It was in that moment that I finally admitted to myself just how seductive I found her. She had set my heart racing from the first time I saw her. Then she said, 'You're a big boy; you're a man now. Surely you can keep a secret.'

The spark in my groin became a flame and I could feel the tension between our bodies, but I could not so much as raise my hand to touch her – my uncle's wife. I couldn't live with that. I broke the spell and looked away, my chest still heaving.

Her right hand reached out and touched my face, trying to reinitiate the spell. 'Why? Don't you find me attractive? After all, I am only two years older than you – that's nothing,' she said, leaning over and whispering in my ear, as though fearing the night outside might carry her words to my uncle. 'I am prepared to give you the best night of your life, and nobody will ever know. I promise.'

'But-but aunty, I can't do it. I want but–'

'Yes. You want.'

'No. I mean I don't want.'

Her hands retreated with an urgency, almost as if my uncle had walked in on us. Her head dropped. She looked like a withering flower. Dry.

'I should tell you something else. You need to know,' she said, raising her head and sliding away so that there was space between us again. 'Your uncle wants a child. He says he'll marry another woman if things don't change soon. He, and everything he has to his name, that's all I have. I can't stand the idea of another woman.' Silence. 'I have fought for you. Please fight for me. I'll leave my bedroom door unlocked. Think about what I've told you and when you're done,' she looked me in the eye, 'come to my bedroom. I will be waiting.' And with that, she stood up and left.

I don't know how to describe my frame of mind even as I remained seated – or suspended – there, except that I felt the full weight of the world pressing down on my shoulders, breaking my back. I must admit that when I finally stood up and took some steps I actually went back and forth between my bedroom and hers several times, and, against my every prompting, I dragged the blue balls to my room.

Next morning she did not respond to my greeting, opting instead to spend much of the day in her bedroom. And when my uncle returned that evening, he and my aunt argued. Later, he poured his usual insults on me and told me to enjoy that night as it was to be my last in his house; he was sending me back to the village. This time she did not stand up for me – she looked on with an air of someone whose mind was traversing other planets.

'Please uncle let me stay. This will disturb my education. Please uncle,' I begged. But every plea invited one more insult. It was done – I was done.

After a night of crying, I left. But, strangely, I felt confident in my ability to make it at my village school and was determined to apply for government sponsorship after Grade Twelve.

It all went to plan.

A year after Grade Twelve I became a fully-sponsored student at the University of Zambia (UNZA) in the School of Natural Sciences, where I made it into Medicine at the end of the first academic year. After another year during which I was introduced to the study of medicine at UNZA Main Campus, I joined the School of Medicine at Ridgeway Campus where I finally trained as a medical doctor. In all that time, the village folk and I cut all contact with my uncle, whom the village elders committed into the hands of the ancestors.

III

'Coin, coin, coin, coin. *Nipempako koini.* I'm asking for a coin. Please help. *Nati nipempako koini.*' Then repeat. His voice gets louder.

Yes, news of his business having completely failed reached the village to the pleasure of the elders and most of the village folk but no one could have imagined the sight now before me. I knew it was bad, but surely not this bad. Then somewhere in my subconscious I hear a velvety voice say, 'It is that bad.' An uprush of déjà vu.

I move closer to the beggar so that pedestrians now pass behind me. I bend over and deposit a coin in each of his dark, cracked palms. But the coins falling into the pits of his palms do not interrupt his words or startle him in any way; his mouth continues to take on the now familiar shapes, the sound no more than a sad version of that once raucous voice that hurled insults at me. Then immediately I realise that the life is gone and all that remains is the chant.

Africanus

How terrible – to see the truth when the truth
is only pain to him who sees!

Sophocles

'A gain, what exactly did he tell you?' Cynthia asked amid chuckles from Beauty and Kunda.

'He said he'd seen the sun make love to the sea.'

'Uh, Malita, tell us more!'

'Come on guys, it was sweet. He read me Percy Bysshe Shelley's "Love's Philosophy." I loved it! He concluded by saying he'd seen the sun make love to the sea. I thought it utterly creative until I got what he was driving at. I also found out it wasn't part of the original poem. Creative nonetheless.'

'Of course he wanted a piece of your paradise!' Beauty said.

'Chris definitely has a paradise of his own to give; you should open the door. You just might find more beauty in his paradise than he could possibly find in yours. You never know girl! Open your mind,' Kunda charged.

'And the thing about bees?' Cynthia asked.

'Well, he actually said that before he said about the sun and the sea. He said bees were in love with flowers. And that, too, was not part of the original poem.'

'And then?' Kunda probed.

'Can't you see, Kunda? The poor boy wants Malita's nectar!' Beauty said.

The three laughed out loud. Malita smiled demurely. They were in a state of near-dishabille, sitting carefree on two *chitenges* spread next to each other on the drying turf under the umbrella of newly-leafed trees in the parkland at the

University of Zambia (UNZA). Malita wore a white V-neck over a khaki knife-pleated skirt; Cynthia a pink blouson; Beauty an olive-green scoop neck over a maroon lace-trimmed tulip skirt; and Kunda a blue-dotted white shirtdress that went very well with her braids.

Waves of heat continued to throw themselves at the lounging students. Then all at once, a cool breeze beat upon exposed skin as though to reward them for something on this mid-September afternoon. Cynthia and Beauty sighed in appreciation. Malita and Kunda kept their gazes afar, over the Goma Lakes, across the Great East Road into Kalundu suburb. *Expectant gazes*, one might have thought.

'Uhm, guys, some boys are hungry, huh?' Beauty said.

'Why? What are you saying?' Cynthia responded.

'It's that boy over there.' She pointed across the lake towards the office block of the Dean of Students' Affairs. 'He has his books with him; he should be looking at them, right?'

'Yes. So?' Malita chipped in.

'He's been looking hungrily at us for almost an hour now. He wants to eat but he can't kill – he's a scavenger. He can't handle this,' she said, rubbing her hands on the outside of her thighs, an act which only seemed to have exposed something more because the boy now ogled her. Then, as though by a sheer might of will, he redirected his eyes to his books. 'I'm sure he's just like Chris!'

'Oh, please give it up!' Malita retorted.

'Okay, now let's be serious,' Cynthia said. 'Malita, are you going to give Chris a chance? I'm sure the guy means well. Besides, he has muscles – you know – and a six-pack just for you!'

The girls laughed. If laughter were dollars, these girls would have had the world's richest on their payroll. They always found something to laugh about; they even laughed at things that weren't funny, just for not being funny. Their space was bereft of secrets. (Malita knew this, and it made her uneasy at times.) Beauty and Cynthia always talked about and looked forward to their weekends; great weekends, thanks to their *Landlords*.

Kunda would often talk about her rich Adonis, the spoilt nephew of the Chief Justice, and how good he was at 'grinding it,' the final-year student who made sure everyone knew that his surname was the exact same one the Chief Justice used, the rogue boy who had forced his first-year room-mate to sublet his bed space to him so he could live like a king, the one who had erased 'Africa 6-21' from the outside of his door and replaced it with a wooden plaque that said 'King 1.' The girls often talked about Kunda's reaction after her first night at the *Ruins*: 'Guys, Fred's a king. He does everything like a king. He ground it, and I felt like a queen. I don't even remember when we stopped. I want more. And I can tell you the exact number of those square boxes in the ceiling,' she had said; to which Beauty had responded, to Cynthia's approval, 'It's great the guy loves you right – oh, I should say the wrong guy loves you right. Nobody but you expected Fred to turn out right. Girl, you have really charmed him. And on grinding it, I'm sure he can learn a thing or two from our *Landlords*.'

'Malita, we are now in fourth year; I don't see why you should be rusting among serviced company. If anything, just get service from the guy. Do you mean that, for two years now,' Cynthia punctuated the rest for emphasis, 'all the graphic talk of our grinding adventures have done nothing to excite you between the legs and cause you to seek escapades of your own?'

Beauty and Kunda looked fixedly at Malita, their eyebrows raised, examining her face for elusive clues and waiting for her full lips to open.

'Well, guys, to be honest,' Malita frowned and appeared to be willing words out of the lakes, 'the *grinding it* talk really does its job, but you know very well that I'm engaged – engaged when a child. My betrothed and his people, and my people, are expecting me to go back to him. They emphasise faithfulness. Come on guys don't look at me like that! It doesn't excite me – I mean the engagement thing. That's why for almost two years now I haven't gone home! I miss my mum, my dad, and my sister but I now feel caged in the village. I want to be free, too, but not with a *Landlord*.'

Faces condensed to pity laced, ever so slightly, with excitement.

'How come you're only saying it now – that it doesn't excite you?' Beauty asked.

'Yes, Malita, you made us all think your engagement excited you. I'm your room-mate and you never confided in me?' Kunda wondered.

'I'm very sorry guys, but I like to be sure of things first. You know how we girls can be impulsive.'

'So, are you giving Chris a chance? Besides, your betrothed, does he have a degree?' Cynthia enquired not so innocently.

They all laughed.

'Of course he doesn't. But it's not about a degree, you know.'

'And Chris?'

'Cynthia, Chris is a nice guy, yes, and he's poetic, yes, but I feel nothing for him. I want to be true to myself before I'm true to someone else. Dad always tells me that I came first for a reason, and that I have to be true to myself and show my little sister the way. He's proud of me – and so is mum. I'm the only one to have come to UNZA and I'll be the only one with a degree in my village – and in the whole chiefdom. I'm famous there, you understand? Hey, I don't even know what I'm saying now.'

'It must be great to be in your shoes! I want to be famous,' Beauty said.

'Okay. So, what next?' Cynthia asked.

'Yeah! What next?' Kunda compounded the pressure.

Another episode of cool air washed over them. They must have been doing something right. The lakes' surfaces rippled. The sun now seemed to be *making love* to the lakes. One small ripple gained momentum and appeared to be taking on the stature of a small wave, but it died a ripple. The lakes always had an especially calming effect on Malita, something she couldn't explain. Only that it reminded her of home, a pristine habitat where she felt closest to nature – even one with it. There, she felt the heartbeat of the land and enjoyed the stream that was its pulse, a constantly running stream, the symbol of life.

A fluttering sounded in the tree branches above. The girls peered up, trying to locate the intruder. A wet paste splotched Malita's forehead, its oozing creaminess nearly trickling into her eyes. Facing down, she grabbed for the free end of the *chitenge* and wiped her forehead. The intruder flew off, and then silence.

The girls laughed.

'Malita, you'll wash my *chitenge*!' Kunda said.

'It must be great to be in your shoes, but I don't want to be shat on,' Beauty said.

'They say it's good luck when a bird shits on you,' Cynthia said. 'And there's still some shit on your hairline; good for your Afro, I guess.'

'It should have shat on your *Brazilians*,' Malita said, looking at Beauty and Cynthia.

'You're in luck, somebody always moves around with baby wipes – scented baby wipes!' Beauty said.

They looked at Kunda, who smiled and handed Malita two wipes. 'Here you are. Your forehead will be cleaner even than before the shit.'

'I'm curious,' Beauty started, 'why do you always have baby wipes on you? Are you permanently ready to welcome a baby? Don't you have a gestation period like us normal people?'

'And what do you mean by "normal people"? Are you saying I'm not normal?' Kunda asked confrontationally.

'Typical, typical, typical African! That wasn't even the question. Remove that phrase and you will still have questions to answer!' Beauty charged.

'Come on guys, give it a rest!' Malita implored.

'Yeah, knock it off! It's a no-brainer; she obviously wants to stay fresh for when it's time to count the boxes on the ceiling,' Cynthia said. 'And who knows! It's also probably part of the drill for this sort of time, you know – Malita and the shit. Besides, I now think all ladies must carry scented baby wipes – without fail!'

II

The coolness, heedless of season, of this place brings an indescribable calm and assurance upon the people of Daku chiefdom. The meandering stream, snaking through forest and savannah as old as the land, flows peacefully, uncomplaining, day and night, separating the three villages on one side of the chiefdom from the four on the other. Young girls of initiation age and newly married women come in their numbers to the stream for water, and to exchange pleasantries and share counsel. Some come singing, dip their buckets into the stream singing, and go away singing sweet songs that arouse the envy of birds. Sometimes, bold birds join in regardless, and the sound graduates from pleasantly vocal to entrancing when accompanied by the grasses, the trees, and the stream, backed by the wind. Yes, the stream sings – and those who spend quiet time here, and have open ears, testify to this. It's as if souls are transformed, healed and cleansed, and have their harmonies upgraded in this domain. It's believed *Mulungu* placed *kamumana* in this place specifically for the people of the Daku chiefdom. The stream is more than a symbol of unity, progress and eternal life: it also, according to the elders, provides a cathartic experience to open souls, and is the confluence of the spiritual and the physical realms.

She's sure her soul is open. She waits for her catharsis, her change. She stills all the sweet sounds of girls on both sides of *kamumana*, closes her eyes and visualises herself opening her soul and ears to the stream. She hears the rushing water, but she wants more. She wants the stream to sing into her being; she wants to feel it. Nothing. She searches for her spirit, in her self-imposed vision, but to no avail. A hand shakes her hard by the shoulder. Her futile reverie is ended.

'Lita! Lita!'

She's back in the corporeal realm. All the sounds and sights she had shut out come at her in full measure. She turns her head and stares, startled, at the equally startled Milika, her little sister, standing behind her.

'Oh, sorry. But, Mili, why did you shake me so violently? I almost fell into the stream.'

'We dipped our buckets at the same time. I scooped my bucketful. Your bucket was still in there. I was talking to you; you weren't responding. Next thing I saw your eyes were closed and you seemed frozen in your crouched position. I got scared!' Milika lowered her voice, 'I thought it was that thing…Muzenge's thing…you know. They say it's his grandfather…you know…his dead grandfather. And–'

'Relax, Mili, I'm fine. I was only thinking.'

Something happened last year that made Muzenge (one of the initiate boys from across the stream) infamous throughout Daku. They say he left his friends, who had brought cattle downstream to drink, and went instead upstream, where drinking water was fetched, to charm his long-time admired, whom he had trailed from home. The girls were surprised to see a boy upstream as it was traditionally designated for females, their *bedroom*; the place naturally oozed with femininity and a boy encroaching on it was taboo. Muzenge was not to be deterred; he was out to impress.

In what seems to be an exaggeration, they say that when he finally stopped in front of the dumbfounded girl standing beside the stream and began to sing his heart out for love, the girl became dazed and fell to her knees, *kamumana* stopped running, birds disappeared from the towering trees, everybody became like statues, the air also stopped, everything stopped to witness the madness. And nobody had prepared for what was to come: the boy stopped mid-song; his every feature froze for what seemed like forever, his eyes rolled upward, white foam started exuding from the corners of his mouth, and then as unexpected as all this he fell into fierce paroxysms all the way down into the stream. They say everything immediately unfroze, and the stream carried the ferociously fitting Muzenge downstream where the deft hands of his friends pulled him out to safety. Bar the fame, it's not clear what followed after that.

'I don't like it! Is that the way they taught you to think at UNZA? Is that the way people think in Lusaka? People should be scared just because you're thinking! It's weird.'

'Come on Mili! Don't you blink? I was only blinking. I blink slowly when I'm thinking.'

It's easy to be famous in Daku. All one needs is to do one thing (completely sublime or totally ridiculous) and their name is in the awareness of Chief Jumbe, who, in the council meetings, repeatedly holds aloft the families from which the names come as shining examples for others to follow, or to shun as in the case of the ridiculous. Milika chose to do the sublime by obtaining seven-points at grade twelve last year (at the same boarding school in Chipata where, six years ago, Malita got eight-points). And, as happened with Malita, the Daku families have been ordered to contribute one chicken each, which will be sold and the money so realised directed towards meeting some of the UNZA fees; it's a given she'll be government-sponsored.

'I hope I never learn to think like you when I go to UNZA. I even thought you'd forgotten how to fetch water from the stream – after two years of not visiting us.'

Malita scoops the water and puts the bucket on her head. Milika puts her bucket on her head, too. They start off for the village, leaving the stream and its enchantment behind.

'I told you I was busy. Students get busy; very busy. You'll see. And I also had to do TP.'

'What's TP?'

'Teaching Practice; it's something School of Education students – those studying teaching courses – do at the end of their studies to get their certificates.'

Milika stops suddenly. Some of her water spills onto her chest, causing her pink *chitenge* dress to cling so tightly to her taut, pointed things and reveal their outline. She has a questioning look on her face.

'Why did you stop like that?' Malita complains sharply. 'You almost made me spill my water. Is something crossing our path?'

'No. Of course not. It's just that everybody thinks you got a degree. I don't get it – you went away all those years for a certificate?'

Malita, realising the reason for the abrupt halt, laughs.

'What? Do I look funny?' asked Milika, puzzled.

'No–'

'Sorry, excuse us! Lita, Mili, how are you?' says the older-looking of three girls as they approach.

'We're fine. How are you?' Malita asks in return.

'We are fine too. Thank you.'

Malita and Milika step into the underbrush to give way to the girls, who overtake them, each artfully balancing a bucket on her head. They are a joy to behold, as their buttocks swing from side to side in what a city boy would think is a premeditated ploy to capture his attention. They dance on until the tall grass conceals them where the path winds away.

'Yes now you look funny.' Malita continues the interrupted dialogue.

'So explain to me about the certificate,' Milika appeals, a little put out at having been laughed at.

'Listen, Mili, when a person passes an academic or professional course, they get certified. This is to show that they've successfully completed a course or programme – whatever it may be. So, yes, I got my degree – my degree certificate.'

'Oh, I see!'

'Good! Now, let's go, shall we?'

'Yes.'

Milika resumes her walk; Malita falls into step behind her.

'Malita. Remember, you once told me you didn't want to teach at a secondary school, have you changed your mind?'

'No. I haven't.'

'So, what are you going to do instead?'

'I'll write.'

'Write what?'

'Fiction. Short stories and novels.'

'Really?'

'Yes, really.'

'Uhm, like Chinua Achebe and Ngugi wa Thiong'o? Teacher made us read *Things Fall Apart* and *The River Between* in literature lessons – it was great!'

'Yeah, something like that, Mili, but more like Namwali Serpell, Petina Gappah, and Chimamanda Ngozi Adichie.'

'Uhm, I don't know those.'

'You'll know them soon.'

Walking behind Milika, Malita appreciates how much her little sister has grown, how much she has blossomed. Her dress clings to her curvaceous body. Her midnight-black Afro hairstyle reminds Malita of her younger self. It must be in the family. Milika throws those light, celestial steps onto the path, one after the other, much more gracefully than the three girls who overtook them earlier. Milika appears not to walk on the ground, like humans, more as if she's gliding on air.

She's ready for UNZA, Malita thinks, *but is she ready for the big decisions that a girl sometimes has to make while there?*

III

The New Education Lecture Theatre was especially baking. The air cons were dead. Most female students were near nude in their outfits. Male students, on the other hand, did not seem to exaggerate the extent of the heat, though there were a few who wore flip-flops, shorts, muscle shirts and vests. It was an hour before noon and the lecture was about to start. The lecture theatre was like a rally with students still pouring in unmindful that it was full and all the seats taken. It was common to have students standing at the back against the wall or sitting in the passageways. It was, after all, Dr Monga's lecture.

He had a way with students, one that other lecturers envied. He knew how to draw the line between informality and formality, and most students confided in, and sought counsel from him. He made literature come alive. His words were refined thought, his gestures distilled intent; he sounded like an excellently-written book. And they loved him, for he inspired them. And because he avoided wearing formal shirts and suits, preferring instead loose, brightly-coloured dashikis, insisting they made him feel more African, most of his students called him 'Africanus,' and he appeared rather encouraging of it – it was his way.

Malita liked sitting in the first row of the middle section, and she was always early to make sure she got 'her' seat. Well, except once when she was late and had to endure the lecture sitting in the passageway, far removed from the *experience* of the front row. She knew her friends also liked everything about these lectures. What she was not sure of was if they liked it as much as she, but they always sat together, absorbing Dr Monga's polished lyrics and condensed body movements. She and her friends always had something to talk about after his lectures.

A hush fell over the crammed theatre. There he was, standing in front of them: of a slight build and a confident face, and of course in one of his many dashikis. In truth, there wasn't much to like in his appearance, but he had a bubbly character together with a commanding presence. It was perhaps something in the way he talked coupled with his lens for viewing life that did the trick. Whatever it was, it worked.

'Welcome everyone!' he said, proceeding to scrawl on the whiteboard: *Oedipus the King*. 'Today we're going deeper into Greek mythology.' He paused to clear his throat. 'What on earth would make someone commit a corrupt deed of the most monstrous kind? Can somebody tell us?'

A hand quickly went up behind Malita.

'Yes?'

'Greed!'

'Do you want to explain, Miss?'

'Uhm, yes. If one wants to have everything good for themselves, they'll indeed commit any sort of corrupt deed to reach that end.'

'Very good, Miss! I admire your logic, but that isn't the answer I'm looking for.'

Kunda raised her hand and said the word she knew Africanus liked, 'Hubris! I can explain. If one has hubris and there's a challenge to that hubris, they'll commit unimaginable corrupt deeds to safeguard that hubris. Especially men; this is usually their character flaw, they have too much unmitigated hubris.'

'Careful Miss Hubris, you're addressing a man!' Dr Monga broke into a laugh, and the theatre did likewise. 'But, I must admit that on a different day your logic would have done the job!'

Malita raised her hand.

'Yes, Lady!'

She was nonplussed at this address. She'd never heard him reference a female, bar some in books, as Lady. Apart from her friends who looked at her enquiringly, nobody else appeared to have noticed the awkwardness of the address.

'I don't claim to know what you're looking for, but I'll give it a try.'

'Yes. You may go on.'

'It's beginning to seem to me – and thanks to the two tries earlier – that the kind of answer you're looking for is one that doesn't necessarily lay the blame on a character, but rather on circumstance.'

'Uhm, interesting! Do you want to clarify?'

'I don't think I can.'

'Well, give it a try.'

'Ah, okay. I would say that the commission of whatever the heinous corrupt deed is, can be influenced by something external, maybe the environment, as opposed to a character's internal promptings. For example, if a fire started in here–'

'Careful Miss, it's already hot in here!'

Moderate laughter broke out. She was disappointed he didn't call her *Lady*. Maybe he'd forgotten.

'Yes Miss, carry on,' he prompted.

'I was saying if, for example, a fire started in here, we would all run out of this lecture not because we want to leave before time but because the situation around us demands that we leave. So, the environment can make people do unreasonable things.'

'Thanks Miss. That's more like it!'

There was applause in the theatre. Even her friends clapped.

'Good! Bring it down now, bring it down. On that premise, we shall now delve into laying the foundation for our discussion. Today I'm only introducing this topic, giving you the general feel of it for an in-depth discussion when next we meet. Oedipus the King, a character of pathos, cursed by the gods. One might think the whole pantheon of Greek gods had cursed him, for his curse was great. And that leads us to *fate*: the fact, at least in Greek mythology and in most other literary works, that our lives and how we conclude them have already been determined by the gods, and that everything we try to do to eschew that determination only brings it upon us earlier than intended; that we're born to go through the motions set by the gods: righteous or evil.

'To get to it, Oedipus was cursed from birth. The motion set for him, of course by the gods, was to kill his father and marry his mother.'

A deep voice buzzed from the blackness of the upper reaches of the theatre, 'And to have children with her?'

'Yes, indeed. Imagine the agony when he finally discovered that he had killed his father, and that his beloved wife was his own mother.'

A sea of bewildered faces filled the auditorium.

'Today, I want us to discuss *fate*, and I want to hear your views.'

Several hands went up.

IV

Night fell upon UNZA. Malita and Kunda were in their room, studying and listening to Hot FM. She felt she had to open up to Kunda about her confused feelings for a man old enough to be her father. She cleared her throat.

'Kunda.'

'Yeah.'

'I haven't shared with anyone, but I think I like someone.'

'Wow! I'm listening. Is it Chris? Who's the lucky guy?'

'It's crazy, very crazy, but if Africanus made a move on me, I don't think I would have the resolve to say no.'

'Uhm, not many girls would actually say this, but I think most of us female students feel that way. And you know how proud he is of his never-married label, huh? Wait until Cynthia and Beauty hear this!'

'Yeah. Don't tell them though. I'll tell them myself if I have to.'

'Malita, I think I know what you feel: a fantasy thing right? Not that it could actually happen. And that *Lady* thing today in class?'

'It's crazy, Kunda, because unlike some girls, I actually want him to make a move, but I'm also scared. And the *Lady* thing? Let's face it, it was a mistake. Funny thing is I felt offended when he later called me Miss.'

'Uhm, sounds like you want to become his *Lady* and get physical with him. But, you know he wants nothing to do with girls. He's a real *monk*, not like these boy-*monks* who are only waiting for an opportunity to *demonk*.'

Malita laughed diffidently. 'You saw when he called me outside the foyer of the lecture theatre?'

'I saw him talking to you. And what was that about? I thought he was saying hi or something.'

'Yeah. But also that he liked my logic, and that I should go to his office tomorrow around the time he usually leaves – don't you find it strange, that I should go to his office? It excites me as much as it scares me. I don't know what to expect.'

'Well, it's very strange! Very strange! But maybe he wants to give you things to read to enhance your logic. I guess the only way to find out is to go there tomorrow. Don't worry, he is definitely not a rapist; he is a *monk*, remember that!'

'Yeah, I will.'

What Malita did not tell Kunda is that she had regarded Africanus, for a long time now, as the ultimate standard of what a real man should be, the quintessence of masculinity, and that it was because of him that she had no interest in UNZA boys. There was, almost, a dark pull to him that she could not explain. She longed to be with him, if only to sit near his talking, moving self. He inspired her in ways that no man other than her father did; he made her want to do more, and become better. Unknown to him, it was because of him that she wanted to come back to UNZA for a Master of Arts in Literature and a PhD afterwards. She wanted to be like him, to teach and inspire like he did. She wanted to tell him exactly how he made her feel, and how much of a better person she was becoming because of him.

V

Nzowa village, blessed with loamy soils and lush vegetation, stands cocooned in that sanctuary-like space amid high hills to the north, west and south, and the stream about a half-kilometre to the east. There are two villages behind the hills to the north and south but Nzowa boasts some of the best thatched-roof mud-brick houses in Daku. Headman Nzowa's house is centrally located, with others dotted randomly around it. There are about as many trees as houses in Nzowa.

It is late afternoon, and Mbata with his wife and Malita are seated under the fig tree outside their home. Something disturbing has come to Mbata's attention.

'My wife, are you serious about this? Do you even know what you're saying?' Mbata asks, concern registering on his face and his few grey hairs appearing to have proliferated in the moment.

'Yes, my husband.'

Mbata, though considered unconventional by his fellow villagers, largely due to the way he embraces the importance of formal education and the way he mentors his daughters, is a man of tradition at heart. He is very good friends with Nkala and wants very much for nothing to come between his daughter and Nkala's boy, Taza. Besides, his good name with the chief for his exceptional *school-learned* daughters would suffer ridicule if he appeared to, at any rate, encourage the abrogation of one of the most important traditions in the chiefdom: betrothal.

He turns to Malita. 'My daughter, you know I only want the best for you and this family. What you want to do will bring disgrace upon us,' he says, his eyes darting between his wife and daughter. 'If I didn't raise you so differently…if you had failed Grade Twelve and had come back here, you would be Taza's wife *as we speak*. Your mother would be holding her grandchild; I would be holding my grandchild.'

'Daddy, I understand your concerns, but I didn't tell mum

why I wasn't going to marry Taza.' She looks at her mother, who now seems thrown, shifting anxiously on the reed mat she shares with her daughter.

'Really?' her mother reacts.

Mbata moves his stool closer to the edge of the reed mat. He clears his throat, leans forward and says, 'Tell us, my daughter, what's going on? Is it that you feel education has created a big gap between you and Taza? Please speak openly.'

Her mother prompts, 'Yes, Malita, tell us.'

'There will be no disgrace upon this family,' Malita insists.

'Please explain,' her father implores.

'Well, yesterday on my way from the stream – I was with Mili – I met Taza. He and I talked for a long time.'

'What did you talk about?' her mother enquires.

'I told him I was going back to school to study for my Master's. He got upset. He said his friends were all married. I told him marriage was the last thing on my mind. He said that was okay because Misodzi would become his wife. He then told me that Misodzi was with child – his child – and that Misodzi's mother knew about it. I now understand why Misodzi has been avoiding me. It's actually good riddance that he has impregnated my best friend because there's no earthly way I could have married him.'

Her parents' faces represent things disjointed, mangled.

'This can't be true, Malita. Misodzi?! I can't believe it. I'm not saying I don't believe you. But, Misodzi?' her mother queries, disbelieving anyway.

'Wait, wait my daughter,' says Mbata, confused. 'Do you mean Misodzi, your friend, is pregnant right now as we speak, and Taza is responsible for it?'

'Yes, father. He said it himself.'

'Uhm. Then…,' Mbata rubs his chin as though searching for answers in his beard, '…in that case, I will have to talk to my friend, and he and I will ask to meet with the headman. I just find it hard to believe that a *good* boy would do such a thing; it's shocking! I'll be back.' He stands, clears his throat twice, and heads in the direction of Nkala's house, hands clasped behind his back, shaking his head.

'Lita, this is very bad,' says her mother. 'But, I guess it makes you happy. You see, Taza is known for only good things in this village. He's definitely the best behaved of all the boys here, and everybody knows it. So, to see him disrespect tradition in this way is beyond me. And if he's not good enough for you, no one is. You know these Daku boys.' She looks at Malita in a knowing way. 'So, tell me, Lita, is there *someone* in Lusaka, maybe at school? Talk to me, I'm your mother.'

'Actually, mum, there is. I was going to tell you, but you're not patient.'

'I'm not. Tell me already.'

'Please, I don't want daddy to know just yet.'

'Don't worry.'

'Fine. There's someone special.'

'Yes, I'm listening.'

'Mum, he's not my age-mate.'

'For as long as he's not younger than you, no problem. We've been seeing this a lot, it's not a problem.'

'Thanks mum.'

'Go on.'

'He's a lecturer.'

'Okay.'

'Yeah. He's madly in love with me. He wants to marry me after my Master's studies. Actually, he is going to pay for my studies.'

'Uhm, so, this lecturer of yours, how old is he?'

'I would say about as old as dad. He's a wonderful man, and I love him! You'll see when you finally meet him. He even wants me to study for a PhD.'

'You seem to really like this man. It's good. Now tell me, your lecturer, what's his name?'

'Doctor Monga.'

'What's his first name?'

'Mum, are you being serious?'

'Okay. Do you have his photo?'

'Yes.'

'May I see it?'

'Of course.'

The sun has already hidden itself behind the hills and soon darkness will enfold the village, accustomed as it is to having the sun wake it up early and send it to bed early.

Malita rushes into the house and returns with two photos; she hands them both to her mother, who draws them closer to her eyes, turns them face-down, and face-up again. Her eyes start to flit between her daughter and the things in her hands. She appears to be using all her strength to hold them up.

Malita is sure she's beginning to see mist in her mother's eyes. She notices that her mother's body is aquiver, with the photos appearing to be taking some strong wind. All is still and the weather is warm, and yet her mother shivers. It makes no sense to Malita.

'Mum, are you all right? Mum, talk to me.'

Her mother is quiet. The shuddering comes to a stop. The photos are still in her hands. Her eyes peer at them as if unable to break away. Malita fears that it could be another Muzenge case. She moves closer to her mother, takes the photos from her, and shakes her by the shoulders. Now, tears pour freely from her mother's eyes. Malita wipes them away with a *chitenge*. Is it possible that the cause of her mother's uncanny behaviour is the photos, the images in the photos? The one shows Africanus in a dashiki, standing in his office behind a large desk, the other is a selfie showing a visibly excited Africanus planting a kiss on the right cheek of an equally excited Malita. She's now sure it's the photos. But why would her mother react like this?

'Mum, what is going on?'

'Lita,' says her mother, steadying herself. 'Has he already *touched* you?'

'Is that why you–?'

'Malita, has he?' she asks, with a doomed finality in her

tone. 'Tell me the truth!'

'Ye-yes, mother.'

'There was once a boy who liked me when I was Mili's age. I was a boarder at David Kaunda Secondary School in Lusaka. I actually think I liked him before he even got to know me. He and I got *seriously involved* by the end of Grade Twelve. We were madly, madly in love; we wanted to spend forever together. I don't know why but our friends called us *Romeo and Juliet*. I told him about my betrothal, and that I was going to be forced to marry my betrothed. He cried – we both cried. We were only children; we couldn't do anything about it. He promised two things: to study all his life, and never to marry. His family was in Lusaka, mine was here. So when it was time to leave school, we parted company. And I ended up here where they made me marry your father.'

'Okay, mum, but honestly you're freaking me out! Let's do away with anecdotes and get straight to the point. You married my father, and he's a wonderful man; so, what's the problem?'

'He is not your father, Malita. And I've never told anyone this, even he doesn't know – so please keep it to yourself. But, with my very young pregnancy from school, I went straight into marriage with your father.'

Malita is mystified. Why is her mother telling her all this? It's not information that will help anyone. Already, she knows that things will never be the same again between her and her parents.

'But, mum, why are you telling me all this? You should have just kept quiet about it.'

'No, my daughter, I couldn't have.'

'Why?'

'Because your father is the man in those photos!'

VI

The depth of night intensifies her hell. Her sister is sleeping, snoring lightly, but Malita is awake and lies motionless in her bed. Her pillow is wet. The lantern is out, the room is illuminated only by the moonlight that streams in through the two small windows in the mud wall. Her eyes are open, they have given up crying or her body has no more tears, she doesn't really care which; they stare vacantly at the poles that keep the thatched roof in place, refusing to close as though forcing her to behold what she desperately doesn't want to see, causing her to gaze at something long enough to *un*see it. It's the cold, unblinking, grotesque gaze of the dead, but her mind is awake and her heart still beats. Her ripple of consequence.

She feels her soul opening – rendering itself welcome to any sort of healing. Maybe it's now time to hear the stream sing; she'll go there at first light, to try and understand her *fate*. She knows she'll never accept Africanus for her father; she'll forever regard her mother's husband as her father.

How will her friends react when they learn that their beloved Africanus, that man who has deflowered her and who is responsible for her budding pregnancy, is her real father? Do her friends really need to know?

And Africanus? What can he do? What *will* he do?

What have I done to deserve this? Malita thinks. *Is there a way to undo what has been done, to unlove one's first and only true love?*

What has been done comes upon her as relentless remembrances: warm breath upon warm breath, heat upon heat, masculine hardness and dominance upon feminine softness and grace, unspeakable pleasure upon ephemeral pain, caress upon caress.

Man of God

The two principles of truth, reason and senses, are not only both not genuine, but are engaged in mutual deception. The senses deceive reason through false appearances, and the senses are disturbed by passions, which produce false impressions.

Blaise Pascal

He looks at her with the eyes of one forced to look at the phlegmy spittle of a TB patient. He hardly recognises her. How a piece of new information can change everything! There she is, seated on that very sofa that bore the weight of their first round of carnal pyrotechnics. The matching brown carpet appears as peaceful as it did when it embraced their utterly spent, stark naked selves. Her eyes, obsessed by the carpet as though recalling the first time, avoid his. He wonders why such an attractive woman could have such an ugly soul, whose ilk he thought were only alive in fiction.

Now it eschews his, the face he always wanted to wake up next to every morning. How, like ice, he melted when their eyes first locked after that church service, how ersatz his life had felt before his heart was touched by hers! There was something unfamiliar and inviting about her, and he couldn't resist it. He knew it had to be her, and he felt justified for the bliss they would later share. If he met her today, he would marry her – and all over again. It's only been a year since he first heard the sofa screech, and now this.

Jack, Jack, Jack! My dear Jack, you don't understand. Even though my eyes are staring at the carpet, I see you looking at me. I feel your eyes all over my hair, the hair you ran your fingers through just last night. Those eyes, your eyes, the same ones that melted into mine, are now crawling all over my body, they slither more sinuously than a snake, and it's how I know you see not my clothes but my soul. But if you see my soul, why are you so angry like a volcanic mountain? Oh, is my soul too complex for your examination? Please look at my heart – is it deceitful? Please look inside…please!

The fan in the corner of the living room hums and hums on this hellishly hot afternoon, circulating heat and a heaviness that's becoming more suffocating by the minute. The curtains, blowing and dancing a little in the circulation, appear as if they are readying themselves to fly away, to leave this mess behind. The wall clock protests thickly...*tuck, tuck, tuck!* He imagines the grey paint on the walls flaking off, the colour they put there together. This room knew them before the bedroom did, and seeing them like this must be an eyesore. His stomach growls, but he doesn't care if it's hungry.

There's a big, menacing-looking fly on the wall just above and behind Christa. While he sees two flies being blown away by the fan, this one only shakes a little when the fan's on it and remains as though undisturbed. It looks determined, like it's on a serious mission.

His eyes move from the fly back to her. He wishes he were her head to carry her thoughts and know each one and follow its intent to the heart, to know if she is in full charge of herself, to know if the person she's become has any roots in her soul.

Jack, why are your hands shaking? Don't lie! The last time they shook like that you ended up punching someone in the chest. You remember that bus conductor who almost cheated us out of our change – how he stammered and fell backwards before giving us our money? I imagined seeing his tail between his legs. Subdued.

But Jack, draw back that anger from your hands – I'm for kissing, not punching. I'm for tender things. Love. Like where we went last night, do you remember? We had wings and flew over places of wonder and lingered a while longer in the most beautiful. We saw the most amazing mountains and rivers, green valleys, birds, and bliss – yes, we saw bliss. And do you remember the waterfall after we flew over the moon? Well, that waterfall was the culmination of it all, the climax: water falling on rocks, the splashes, the rain, the rainbow. That, Jack, is my definition of bliss. Blissful. Love. We must be ready to die for that, right? Are you afraid of dying, in the ambience of bliss? Oh, no, I feel your eyes on me again.

A dry cough rips through the thickets of heat and swamps of heaviness, the fly is perturbed. The pastor rubs his mouth with the back of his left hand. What's wrong with him? Where has his cough come from? He was jumping and sweating on the pulpit just yesterday, as his message on Job literally galvanised those whose faith had started to dry and fall by the wayside. It was that message and the eventual blessings Job received that made Jack dig into his *bombasa* to retrieve and offer the last bit of his money. He didn't think about it, it just happened. It's good to endure for a moment, we are just passing by after all. Pilgrims.

No, it's not because of the offering that the pastor is here today. Jack called him this morning to help resolve a serious matter in this thing he himself put together before God and man. The sentence. And that he decided to come here in the afternoon is absurd because, by now, the bitter swell that brought them together has evidently festered.

Another cough, but this time it's a whooping cough. The pastor's coughing is changing gears. No, he didn't have the merest hint of a cough yesterday. He was his ever-energetic self, smiling widely like his mouth was given to helping the sun shine while he greeted his congregants outside the building after the service, repeatedly saying, 'Praise God! Praise God,' and 'God bless you! God bless you!'

Today, clad in a black Fortini Milano eight-button Chinese collar suit, with a hint of pure white just below his Adam's apple, and shiny, pointy black shoes, he looks lost and his clothes borrowed. He may look lost but the clothes are surely his. Perhaps his mojo doesn't thrive in such a milieu, one awash with suspicion and anger. Well, it's his job to provide a solution. That is, after all, his calling: to bring comfort where there's discomfort, a resolution where there's conflict, an answer where there's a question.

The pastor is uneasy. He doesn't know why he can't fully compose himself before this couple. He tries, to no avail, to muzzle the soft voice in his head that says he's part of the problem he's been called to solve. He shifts uneasily in his seat, looking like he's about to ask permission to leave. His eyes are on Jack who says, 'Yes, man of God, I called you because as you know, we have to seek your intervention before anyone else's if and when we have a problem. Well, we do have – I don't know how to say this – a very serious problem.'

What Jack doesn't see is the anger in Christa's eyes that's now suffused her entire face. If only the carpet could talk!

Intervention – intervention? Jack, what makes you so sure that interventions are innocent? Aren't you supposed to make sure that an intervention didn't cause the problem in the first place?

The pastor says, 'It is a wise thing you have done, my son, to keep things within the church. Yes, marriage can be tricky sometimes – it comes with all the beauty of it. I counselled you in your preparation for this union; make no mistake, I'm on hand to counsel you further. So, let me hear it.'

Christa has only love and pity for Jack, and only hate and anger for the pastor.

Jack, his whole body shaking, says, 'I-I-I'm positive…HIV-positive. I've been repeatedly feverish of late, and I mentioned it to you yesterday, so I went to the hospital for a check-up. I suspected malaria. They broke the news. I couldn't believe it. I still can't believe it. I took my wife – she's positive, too. They counselled us, man of God; they counselled us. They said we should stick together. I love my wife, but I need to know the truth – the whole truth! She's the only woman I've known my whole life, but she insists I gave her the virus. She also insists I'm the only man she's known. Oh, I'm finished…I'm completely finished!' He buries his head in his hands.

The pastor, his voice sounding weak and nervy, enquires, 'Do you mean HIV? HIV like AIDS – HIV/AIDS?'

'Yes, man of God, AIDS!'

The pastor opens his mouth but he can't find the words. His eyes have never opened wider, his heart begins to explode against his ribs, as his brain goes to work on an array of church files, gone and around, ranging from married to unmarried females across several committees, to the Choir and the Praise Team: Lizzie, Naomi, Sarah, Mukupa, Cynthia, Taona, Beauty, Fanny, and Michelo. Which one? His years of *play* come at him like an unremitting flood. He thinks of his lovely wife. His whole body quivers under the suit, as he struggles to compose himself. He knows he's got to get himself together.

Jack continues, 'Yes, man of God. I told you during one of those counselling sessions that she was going to be my first and only woman. Did I keep myself chaste for this?' He looks at his wife. 'Oh, Christa you have killed me!'

The pastor says, 'Okay...I'm sure you were told about treatment....'

'Man of God, please...I need you to ask my wife to say the truth. Please!' Jack interrupts.

The Pastor is deep in thought, *Christa, oh my dear Christa! I'm so sorry. I'm sure you know I never meant for such an outcome for you, for us; I could never wish it in a thousand years. I know I told you that you were the only one apart from my wife and that it would always be that way; and of course you found out later it wasn't true. I desperately wish I'd stayed true. But wait, it's possible I had already contracted the virus when I took your virginity, and those two other times before your wedding served only to ensure we shared it.*

'Please, man of God,' Jack begs, his voice childlike, as he begins to move off the edge of his seat onto his knees.

'No, no! Please don't kneel, I'm your servant. Please get back to your seat.'

Jack retakes the edge of his seat. He doesn't know it but his behind is numb and it's imploring him to move it to the soft middle of the seat. He pays it no attention. He sits there hardly looking at his wife, whom he now loves and hates in equal measure.

'Together, Jack,' says the pastor, 'we shall find a solution. I don't want you to dwell so much on thinking your wife gave it to you or that she's been unfaithful. During my many years in ministry, I've counselled many couples who were on the verge of divorce because of this sort of situation. I'm not supposed to be telling you this, counselling sessions and their content are meant to be confidential. Anyway, I'll not mention names. But some couples – and you know some of them in our church – have accepted their situation with so much calmness you would never know their true state, and they live happy and healthy lives.'

'But, man of God, I just want my wife to be honest with me. Please talk to her.'

'What did she tell you?'

'That she has no idea where this came from. But....'

'Then you should believe her.'

'But, man of God, where did it come from? I need to know the truth in order to move on with her…the truth. I just know it will set me free. That's why I need you to get it out of her, man of God.'

The pastor thinks, *My dear Christa, how do I begin to ask you this? It's clear that I don't want to ask you what Jack demands. I know you know where it came from, but I don't know who gave it to me. What question shall I ask you? How do I start?*

He looks directly at Jack. 'Is she responding to you?'

'No. Not since several hours ago.'

'It's clear to me that your wife is in shock. She can't talk right now – she just can't.'

I can talk just fine, you idiot!

'She blames you for this, Jack. I know it's strange. But, trust me, she's in shock because she knows absolutely nothing about where it came from. So, instead of piling unnecessary pressure on her that can even plunge her into depression, the two of you have to accept the situation and move on. There are many ways to contract this virus; you can contract it through use of infected and unsterilized instruments that come into contact with blood, like a razor blade or a needle; sometimes through blood transfusion. And I feel it in my spirit that your case has nothing to do with premarital or extramarital sex.'

Jack's face begins to soften. He thinks he's being unfair to Christa. Maybe HIV just happened upon them, or one of them – even both of them – used an infected blade. He has to believe the man of God, his 'spiritual father.'

Christa's gaze burns into the carpet. *I have magma of my own, and I wish I could spew it all on you. Ntss! I can melt you to the bone, Godfrey. 'Man of God' my foot! I don't know what I saw in you. I guess you were just an experiment, a toy. I was infatuated with you, yes. But it all died when I first looked into Jack's eyes. I found love, and I've been faithful since. But you, you Godfrey, made sure I would not have joy. I want to kill you!*

The pastor clears his throat. 'Be strong my son. We shall pray, and surely God will give you strength to carry on. Remember, God is love. And he who says he knows God but has not love does not know God. You my son, you know God – and if it should even be for that reason alone, you will not stop loving your wife and your marriage will not end. Instead, it will become stronger. This is the devil, can't you see? Remember Job, huh? The devil wants you to stop loving your wife. He wants you to lose hope, to insult God, to die. But no, not you my son – not you. You will not give him the pleasure!'

You are the biggest devil I know. In fact, you are the only devil I know.

Jack settles his behind into the cushion, looking encouraged.

'So, Jack, I shall leave you to apologise to your wife for the way you've treated her. And when you need me, I'm only a call away.'

Jack nods repeatedly, weakly, his denial clearly becoming acceptance.

'We shall now pray. Stay seated. Relax. Open your hearts to love, for God is love.'

The pastor stands up and breaks into a chorus, Jack joins in, Christa's face is half-raised and her lips show soundless movement.

Nasumbula, nasumbula, nasumbula,
(I praise, I praise, I praise)
Nasumbula ishina lyenu mwe Lesa,
(I praise your name God)
Ichikuku chenu mwe Lesa teti ndondolole,
(Your kindness God I can't explain)
Nasumbula ishina lyenu mwe Lesa.
(I praise your name God)

The pastor suddenly raises his arms aloft wailing, 'I feel His presence – the Spirit. He is here. Oh, *shibobo-rakata!*'

Nasantika, nasantika, nasantika,
(I worship, I worship, I worship)
Nasantika ishina lyenu mwe Lesa,
(I worship your name God)
Ukutemwa kwenu mwe Lesa teti ndondolole,
(Your love God I can't explain)
Nasantika ishina Lyenu mwe Lesa.
(I worship your name God)

A worshipful mood takes over. The pastor, transfigured and vibrating, his shoes stomp the carpet and his lips move electrically, shaping a strange language; Jack, his hands raised in surrender and his knees on the carpet, his lips pray, tears trickle down his cheeks from the corners of his closed eyes, as he oscillates gracefully from side to side; Christa, seated and face half-raised, her full lips move slowly – no sound.

Christa is lost in thought, *I have to find a way to get us out of this church – his church. I'm already out, but clearly my husband isn't. He's too devoted. Just look at him now – lost, owned, brainwashed, and saying things he doesn't understand. I'm sorry Jack, but this spiritual father of yours is the devil incarnate.*

Prayers continue in tongues before the pastor brings the spiritual charge to a close. '*Rababababa-shika! Ubodo, ubodo, ubodo kuma-shika rababababa-kumu! Yav-dey vav-hey, yama-shika raba-kumu!* Oh, yes. Oh, yes! Renew their marriage. Oh, yes Holy Spirit. In the name of Jesus. Amen!'

II

The roar of the engine of the pastor's latest Mercedes-Benz saloon permeates the air, as it peels him away to other fish. Jack ambles back into the house to find Christa still in that petrified position. He's ready to apologise. He's going to apologise.

Jack, if I tell you the truth, will you still love me? And of what use will the truth be if it will only serve to hurt you further and cause you to lose the joy of living? Look at you Jack! That church is your life, you believe everything Godfrey tells you, and – I think I'm right – you can die for Godfrey. I see it in your eyes. Godfrey, with his tongues, has a positive effect on you as your anger has completely petered out and you are willing to bury this and live positively with me. You look so stupid right now, hare-brained. I should apologise, not you. But I will not. And one day, I will spew my magma on Godfrey.

The fan hums roughly, like the dying engine of an old truck, swinging from one end to the other and taking a bit longer at the ends as if to avoid witnessing Jack's apology. The fly will have none of it, so it extricates itself from the wall, floats around the dancing grey curtains and out through the open window. The grey paint tries desperately to flake off the walls, and the carpet can hardly bear the weight of the kneeling Jack.

Ire of an Ant

There is no need for ants to have the ability to fly.
Karl Pilkington

I'm here with her only because her widowhood has come after mine. I know from experience the totality of what awaits her, and my mind can't abide the cringeworthy horror of the indignity she's bound to suffer, the sheer inhumanity of it all.

There's an antlike air about her, unassuming but potentially dangerous. You don't see her cry, though she has every reason to. She seems instead to possess a quiet ability to bite back. Or, it's all in my head. It's just that mum once or twice told me she'd witnessed an angry ant kill an elephant. Tall tale. But then, she's full of folklore. I learned later that she hadn't seen any such thing, but the anecdote has stayed in my memory like a stain.

We are strangers forced to share a round pole-and-mud wall with a thatched roof in disrepair. We sit wrapped in *chitenges* on a reed mat, on a mud floor, our heads shaven, bodies slumped, legs straight, buttocks numb. We're kept in darkness – 'The sun must not see them,' they say – and we aren't allowed to talk to each other, so I whisper to her whenever I'm sure no one is at the door.

We have our backs to the wall opposite the door, next to which we've stationed our 'toilet.' And the bucket stinks ever more obnoxiously every time we squat over it. She remains in the hut where the air she breathes is a confluence of smells: sewage and sweat and something like rotting rat, while I go to my daughter after sunset and spend the nights with my new husband only to rejoin her at the lip of sunrise. So I make sure I don't shit in the bucket but she has to as she hasn't any recourse. I think it's less revolting that she handle my pee than my shit when every night – the only time she's allowed to come out – she empties the bucket. She isn't to bathe until a little after sunset on the seventh day.

Vertical streams of light through several gaps in the roof tell me the sun's overhead. And, as though not to be outdone, the stench ups the ante; it's only now, sitting next to her, that I realise she's the source of the 'rotting rat' smell. I crave to bathe her, to show her someone cares. She grabs the 5-litre container and drinks the last of the water, her lips wrap around where the lid was, where her lips have been for days.

The door pushes open, a teenage girl ambles in with the reluctance of a general getting into a war he knows he's bound to lose. The usual two plates of *nshima* and leafy greens. Her only meal of the day. No water. I daren't look too closely, but my best guess is pumpkin leaves. She's used now to eating the meal alone as I've resorted to fasting until I go home. I watch her stretch her right arm, her long spindly fingers form a crater in the centre of the *nshima* and start to shape a morsel, which then goes into the greens and into her mouth. You can't recognise taste in her food but she chews and swallows like it's one of the most delectable meals, as her hand continues to draw the triangle from plate to plate to mouth to plate.

Outside, life maintains its usual shape. Dogs bark, chickens cluck, birds twitter, goats bleat, ducks quack, and from time to time I can hear cattle lowing. Children play and laugh without a care. The sounds of women and their work caress the air: calling children to lunch, thudding of pestle on mortar, clanking of lids on pots, spreading of mats on the ground (I imagine), and repeated calls to children followed by threats of how their fathers will 'discipline' them if they don't come at once. The quiet, deep tones of men in groups rumble ever closer to where women call children, for the calls to children are meant to be loud enough to let the men know it's time to assemble under the fig tree at the centre of the village, a short distance from our hut. The sound of footsteps to and from the tree and women urging their daughters to hurry mark the air, as household by household delivers lunch to be enjoyed by all the men, with the exception of the headman whose status doesn't favour mingling the way of the common man.

So everything is normal and unaffected outside, but it's turning from ridiculous to horrible inside the hut. Comfort is that her ordeal's coming to a close, after which she's to go back to the city and await her fate. And if by any chance she survives, she's to come back and pick a husband. But I want her to talk to me, to tell me if she did what they say she did. And *why*, if at all. Not that it'll change her fate; she's still expected to die by the sinking of the next moon, after the rite tonight, and that's because they think her guilty. I don't see guilt, try as I do, let alone a shred of remorse in her. I see disappointment, brokenness, resignation and a quiet acceptance of her state, but beneath all this, under her crippled humanity, lies a suggestion of lightning whose thunder – I think – will soon resound.

II

My ordeal, even though terrible, was not like hers. When about a year and a half ago my husband died, they didn't think me his murderer. It was clear for all to see he'd been killed by a crocodile. His water-filled body, with a missing right leg severed at the hip, recovered by other fishermen who'd gone to the river that morning, served to the men as a warning to desist from night-fishing alone in a canoe, casting mosquito nets. It was indeed a dangerous upgrade on catching things from mosquitoes to fish, plus deadly and inadvertently, to crocodiles.

On my way to the field that morning I felt no inkling of bad news. Everything appeared ordinary – plus just like every morning, the sun peeped before its full rise. And not having come back home was normal for Matala whenever he'd go 'netting,' for he had a shack near the river where he'd spend those nights to be early enough to pull the nets in the morning. He would join me later in the maize field to help with weeding despite my soft protestations for him to rest. With a smile to melt my heart he'd say, 'Where you are, my love, is where my heart is.'

Footsteps in the distance, getting louder and closer: one of the fishing apprentices, his name Lweta, running after me, panting like a dog. I stopped. I think he thought he was doing me a favour breaking the news to me that way, except the normal procedure should have involved two or three members of the men's council coming to my hut to unwrap the news ever so gently, with a copious measure of practised care. Retrospectively, it wouldn't have helped as it was devastating news all the same; becoming a widow after only three months of marriage was beyond heart-wrenching. No wonder I didn't cry, no wonder my mind refused to accept the new reality that my beloved Matala was gone, that his developing child would be fatherless, that I'd have to forget all the warmth and joy he'd brought to our home, into my life.

It was only after his burial when I found myself secluded in the hut of the cursed, those whose dead husbands still wanted to come back to them and be intimate, that the weight of his death came to bear. My body became a dam and my eyes the spillway gates. All the concentrated emotion started to gush out in ways I'd never thought possible. Even Nina, whose husband had died about a year before, there to unburden on me whatever little connection with the world of the dead she still had, couldn't help but hold me, as we sat on that reed mat, in that same hut known by myriads of ghosts of dead husbands.

Although I was allowed to bathe every night, I still had to spend my days and nights in the hut, eat one poorly cooked meal of *nshima* and leafy greens every day, pee and shit in the bucket. Whenever I could, I'd withhold my shits until after

Nina went to her life after sunset. And I'd remain alone to brave the cold nights in the hut, on the mat, head shaven, a *chitenge* my only clothing and cover. It was hard to sleep on the unforgiving floor. I'd wake with aching bones – a sign, they said, that my husband's ghost was doing its job.

To those grown enough to know things, it was known that the ghost of a husband would come a little after every midnight and violate the widow brutally while she slept; this the ghost did, aware that the seventh day was approaching. On that day the husband's ghost would, after seeing the 'Hand' in action, throw a tantrum and abandon the widow and the world of the living altogether and find a new wife in the world of the spirits.

In cases where a wife had something to do with her husband's death, the ghost wouldn't leave and, having seen the act of the Hand, would smell blood and exact vengeance on the wife by the sinking of the next moon. The wife would die, while the Hand would live on to annoy more ghosts.

Sanctioned by the chief and the medium, at the behest of the gods, and given to service all the twelve villages, 'Hand of the gods' was a position of honour in the spiritual arm of the chiefdom. Our Hand came to his calling, according to what I learned, when he was twenty-five, after the death of the former Hand, breaking the hearts of his parents who had wanted their only son to marry and give them grandchildren. It wasn't enough that they had five grown daughters, three of them already married with children. With an unwilling acceptance, they gave in to the will of the gods. 'It is obvious,' the elders had said, 'that he has no interest in women or marriage. Look at him! His friends are all married men with children. It is clear what his calling is.'

Now middle-aged, his reputation preceded him as a *gifted* Hand, servicing some young widows well beyond the seventh day. I was young and widowed, too, but I cringed at the thought of another man inside me, especially that I was pregnant, and the very thought was betrayal to my beloved

Matala and his unborn child – I'd no sooner hurt them than myself.

My day came. The sun set. Nina went to her life, but she was to join twelve representatives of the men's council and the two guards outside the hut at midnight to escort the Hand to his duty and wait for him to emerge. When I finished bathing and returned to the hut, a small mattress lay on the floor where the mat had been, a clean *chitenge* neatly folded on it, next to a new container of drinking water, and the bucket was gone. I wrapped the clean *chitenge* around me and sat on the softness. It almost felt like home.

In no time, Mama-Ngoza, one of the respected representatives of the women's council, sauntered in, trepidation or empathy on her face. In her hands was a tray which, by the uneasy manner she carried it, appeared heavy, too much for her frail frame. She deposited the tray in front of me without a word – *nshima* with chicken and mushroom, and a small dish half-filled with water. I thought I heard a grunt and her bones crackle, as she squatted and bent her spine to reach the floor. Then she sat next to me on the mattress. The flickering paraffin lamp cast shaky giant shadows of us on the wall and quarter-way across the thatch on poles which together formed a cone above us. Those shadows at the mercy of the flame, I liked their size but disliked their shakiness as I felt that unsteady, that vulnerable, inside. Extinguish the flame, the giants die. Not an option.

I washed my hands in the bowl and started to eat. Still no word. I could hear myself chew and swallow heedless of how silent I wanted to keep things. I heard the wind howl at the cone, everything within and without. I sensed Mama-Ngoza's warmth towards me. She hadn't said a word yet, but her presence began to invigorate me. Scarred as she was with experiences some of which words couldn't carry, I could've sworn she felt all of my fear, shame and worthlessness.

Abruptly, she cleared her throat almost in the manner of men. It nearly made me choke, as I swallowed my last morsel.

'Despair not, my child. Tonight you are to give your body to a man other than your husband. Yes, you'd rather not do it. I understand. But tradition is tradition, my child; it has to be kept, for without it we are nothing, we have nothing. The ways of the gods have to be respected by all.'

I must have imagined it, but her voice seemed to have lost its natural tone, it seemed to catch in her throat, almost like someone or something was breathing down her neck. Perhaps she needed another throat-clearing. No.

'You know the ghost of your husband will not leave you until you give your body to the Hand tonight. You know, also, that I am not here to negotiate anything, I am here to try and make tonight a little easier for you. Besides, I know that you are with child,' she said, looking me square in the face, my heart flipped (how could she tell I was pregnant when I'd only stopped going to the moon a month before?), 'and worrying and refusing to open yourself to the will of the gods will only harm your pregnancy. So, if it will make things any easier when that moment comes, close your eyes and imagine it is your husband.

'Tomorrow morning, at first light, the chosen members of the women's council will escort you back to your normal life. Well,' she opened her hands as if to ask a question, her mouth in a knot and her eyebrows raised, creasing her forehead even more, 'not so normal because you will have to adapt to a life without your husband. But twelve moons from now you will be allowed to take a new husband, and life will be back to normal. Even better if, on the morning you leave here, you choose to become the second wife to Matala's elder brother. And this,' she said, raising her hands and slicing the air above her, 'will be a memory – only a memory – confined within this hut.'

She struck me as sincere. It was, though, the way she said *hut* that made me cringe. It was a sneer, an unsettling whisper, the way the afraid talk about ghosts. No, it was worse – it was as though you lost some of your life every time you said the word, and she'd just lost some of hers. Was she afraid? Because, in truth, she appeared as though she had taken my place, as though I would stand up and leave her in the hut, as though the Hand was to ravage her that night.

Silence.

The story held that the current Hand had ravaged Mama-Ngoza in that selfsame hut when he was only about a year into his service – and she was then in her late sixties. An act whose insult to her dignity, many imagined, she still carried. It was tradition, yes, but she was alleged to have felt violated by this man younger than her own sons.

When she finally spoke, it was as if she was thinking aloud, telling herself, 'A few hours from now, he will come in and do to you as expected. Please think of him not as a man who has been between the legs of countless widows; think of him instead, as, uh, a servant of the gods.' Her last five words didn't come on the same wave as the rest of the sentence.

I wanted to ask her something, to say something, but all the questions in my head refused to form fully and I ended up with bits of what should have been questions, like '...hurt?' '...the ghost?' '...gentle?' I was unable to communicate. Thoughts failed me, and words, like tails, followed on cue.

In my peripheral view, in the lamplight, her profile flickered rapidly between shiny and dim bronze. High cheekbones, full lips, sharp chin, Nubian nose, clear round eyes, and with her grey hair hiding under her headcloth, you could tell how beautiful she must have been at my age. I imagined her skin without wrinkles, her gait elegant. But time having streamed through her for nearly a century, her body now felt its age in earnest.

As Mama-Ngoza struggled to her feet and picked up the tray, ready to leave, it was her shadow that caught my eye: you would have thought that looming so tall and with its head reaching the cone's point it would somehow be stable, yet you had only to focus on its edges to notice it was still wobbly. As she ambled towards the door, I had a strong conviction she needed a hug. Her back to me, she opened the door and, for a brief moment, a breeze swept in on moonlight, the lamp prepared to surrender, but the door closed and I was alone, waiting for my next guest.

Seated on that mattress, back pressed against the wall, I hugged my knees and kept my legs in a constant squeeze as though to keep something from escaping. In that position, lost in time, I heard movement – the guards, then deep tones and many steady footsteps approaching the hut. A pause, everything was still for several seconds, then two feet met the ground one after the other and stopped right at the door. A calm, like one before a storm.

I didn't intend it, I thought I'd be strong, but my eyes welled and a sob shook my body so fiercely as though to exorcise me. The moment had come, and very soon the door would open, perhaps a breeze would sweep in on the moonlight and the lamp would yield, but one thing was for sure: I'd forever be changed.

He stood in the doorway, his muscular torso bare. A giant among men. I could see a group of men at his back. I didn't see Nina but I knew she was there as tradition demanded, and that realisation was just a little soothing, that I wasn't the only woman in the company of men while the village slept, that I could survive this because she had, that her being there said I wasn't alone. The moonlight came alone and the flame stood tall; and when the door closed so assuredly behind him that I didn't imagine it ever opening again, his midnight-black shadow, as he approached the mattress, was unflinching and undaunted, covering the roof in a way that made the point seem absent.

He kicked off his sandals, then peeled his dark *chitenge* from around his waist and let it fall beside him, causing the flame to dance – only in that split second did his shadow appear just a touch shaky. His body really belonged to a man and his hardness, so huge, whose shadow on the wall was a pole, was like nothing I'd ever seen before. It was going to hurt.

Definitely pleased with his presentation and my surprise, a sly smile crept across his face contorting it in the poor lighting. I didn't know whether to stay hunched or discard my *chitenge* and lie supine and get it over with. For the sake of the age-old custom to which all women once widowed surrendered their bodies, I chose the latter.

He showed my quivering body no mercy. Grabbing his hardness and beginning to force his way between my legs without the tenderness of foreplay, he was hurting me, bruising and ripping my flesh, like he was making me a woman. I closed my welling eyes and tried to imagine it was my husband but no, my husband would be gentle, careful to use mirth to lighten the mood and then start with a caress, before touching the right areas, so that heat would spread and my body would want him. Then, and only then, would he ease in – he would never force his way.

Having done much damage, the hardness made it into my body and the Hand began to pound mercilessly, like the way we women would come together in the village square and use pestle and mortar to pound maize for our families. His every thrust was my pain, his every satisfied grunt my indignity. And just as I was going to cover my face, his hands pinned mine to the mattress, so I decided to keep my eyes closed throughout the act to not behold that stupid look on his face that kept inferring, 'I am a man. You're just a woman.'

The whole time I imagined my husband standing against the wall, watching me being ravaged, watching another man take his place. How it must have irked him to see another man drink so carelessly from his well! This was why the elders praised the savage brutality of the Hand; they said he annoyed the ghosts so much they didn't want to return.

I don't remember how long it took before his thrusts intensified and his hips started to dig into me with renewed violence and his body shuddered, but his deep breathing, just before his body slumped on me, told me he'd knocked himself out. I could almost feel his hardness breathe in my sore rawness.

About a minute later, he pulled out and hastened to wear his *chitenge* and sandals. Without a word, he left. The waiting men, with the exception of the guards, broke into chants invoking the gods, reminding them I was now a 'clean' woman, and banishing my husband's ghost.

'Gods of our fathers, you who never sleep, we present to you a clean woman tonight. Please accept her as such.'

'Matala! Matala! You no longer belong to the land of the living and Sepo is no longer your wife.'

'In the name of the gods, your gods, go and take a wife in the spirit world.'

This continued for some time with every man in turn putting in what he thought was a powerful string of words, while the others agreed, 'Yes, it is done,' as though this made the words more powerful, as though the gods would have no choice but to accept me.

Escorted away the following morning, I found I had to go to my parents' house and start over because Ngula, Matala's elder brother, that paunchy drunk, had taken over the house I'd come to know as home for three blissful moons. He made it clear the only way I was to move back in was by becoming his wife, and the women encouraged me to move in with him. But, everything about me was broken and bruised and I knew I needed time to heal. So, I decided to stay with my parents and delay my next move, a development the women tolerated but weren't in any small way supportive of.

Moons rose and sank to rise again and sink, and my parents agreed with me that what happened next in my life was to be of my own volition. About a year later, my heart chose the man who chose me. And, seamlessly, in more ways than I thought he could, Munguni started to fill the void left by Matala. The spring in his gait, the way he put me first, the gentle way in which he spoke to me, the way his eyes drew me in, and the laughter – so similar to Matala's – made me believe that souls could collaborate to achieve the smile of a woman.

III

I try to make small talk with her, to no avail. I've tried all this time but she won't talk to me. I want to tell her about Mbuyeni, the Hand, but how do I if I can't tell if she wants to know? I want to know if she can talk, if she needs me at all.

The hours fly by and the sun sets. As I open the door to leave, I know the next time I'm coming back will be to stand outside the hut, in the company of men, and watch Mbuyeni storm in and do to this frail woman as expected of him by the gods: ravage her so brutally. Standing in the doorway, I turn and look at her bowed head, willing her to look at me, and for the first time she raises her head. I see defeat on her face but her eyes meet mine, show an alien brand of stubbornness, and it's at once clear as day she probably holds an ace. But what could she possibly do? I dismiss her steely eyes as her last line of denial; Mbuyeni, that beast, will surely come and do to her worse than he did to me. It breaks my heart.

IV

Mbuyeni leads the march from the village square to the hut. The night is dead and, from time to time, only the trill of insects fills the air. We march steadily and solemnly as to battle. A few paces from the hut, he stops brusquely. We all stop. The two guards by the door move to stand on either side of us. As they turn to face the hut like the rest of us, Mbuyeni storms in and shuts the door behind him.

My experience with him begins to flood my mind. I wonder how that frail woman is handling things in there. Has she, like I did, opened her legs and let him thrust brutally? Or has she taken one look at his hardness and fainted? Whatever is happening in there, when it's done I'm sure she won't be able to move her body tomorrow morning.

As we stand here like a horde assigned to deliver death to the woman, I hear what sounds like whispers coming from the hut. The men begin to eye one another; you can almost see the question marks float on air. Aside from rotating, shaking and nodding their heads and several throats clearing, no one says a word or initiates any sort of action, even as the whispers that now take on the form of an argument intensify. Yes, there are insect sounds but this isn't a blend of two insects getting intimate. Besides, the Hand isn't to say a word while performing his duty. So, it's inconceivable that he's a party to the whispers.

Suddenly, there's quiet. Perfect stillness. I know my face is releasing questions of its own now. Then a woman's voice permeates the air, moaning. It's the moans of a woman truly enjoying herself, and all the while I hear an urgent whisper – probably Mbuyeni trying to quieten her. I'm sure all of us are embarrassed because our heads begin to bow while our eyes push upward trying to glimpse the embarrassment of others. It gets worse; the moaning gets louder and defiant, without a sign of ending, and every passing minute feels like forever. (Traditionally it is anathema for a woman to show any sort of dominance or produce loud sounds of enjoyment during the act; all girls are made aware of this during their rite of passage into womanhood.)

As if to compound the awkwardness, the moaning increases and becomes vibrant, like of a woman in a powerful moment of orgasm. Pure pleasure. Then a loud scream – the sound of pure pain. And now, instinctively, we rush to the door. A guard kicks it, it yields. I see, through the tiny spaces left by the men's bodies, the woman huddled peacefully in a *chitenge*, her head bowed as though in prayer, and Mbuyeni lying face-up, trying to rein in his screams from a place of sheer agony, his hands trying to put blame on the woman. Before I see more, the rest of the bodies cut in and the door shuts, leaving me outside alone with the guards.

I'm all ears.

'Woman! What have you done to him? You must reverse this.'

'You are a witch, woman. Who sent you to come and disgrace our land?'

'We can do nothing to you, for you now carry the ultimate curse – the curse of the gods.'

'Yes, you should have known that to anyone who harms the Hand in any way is meted out the ultimate curse by the gods themselves.'

'There is no escaping their wrath; no form of intervention by any human or entity can absolve you of their wrath.'

'Woman, you will be dead by the setting of tomorrow's sun.'

This manner of communication continues for a few more moments before one voice says, 'My fellow wise men, let some of us rush the Hand to the headman's house before his condition worsens, lest the gods punish us for neglecting their own.'

The door opens and five men walk out, carrying Mbuyeni in the most careful way they could fathom – one each arm, one each leg, and one with hands under his lower back, his *chitenge* spread over him.

The remaining men walk out and huddle together in the spot Mbuyeni had left us standing, their backs to the hut. Something inside my chest begins to push me towards the partially open door; I start for it and, to my surprise, the guards make no attempt to stop me. Once inside, I find that I don't know what to do, I'm more confused than the men. I want to ask her what she's done to him, that's all, but I know, like before, she won't answer any of my questions; she doesn't even acknowledge my presence. So I just stand and watch her. Then, just as unexpected as the events of the night, she raises her head and looks at me the way she looked at me earlier, only this time to add to her steely eyes are the beginnings of a self-satisfied smirk. I blurt out the question and I haven't a clue where I've found the strength. 'What...?'

'I sat on it,' she says.

I'm not sure if it's that she can actually talk or that she's done what she says she's done that confounds me to the core. I want to ask more, then I hear movement in the distance. Her head returns to a bow. I walk out quickly.

The twelve men approach the hut and one of them orders the woman to come out. They wait. Nothing. The man repeats his call. Another moment passes. They look at one another, as heads shake. Then the door opens fully and she appears, unshod, a *chitenge* her only covering. She doesn't look at the men. It's as though she has emerged from the hut on her own terms. And, as the spokesman begins to open his mouth to banish her from the land and possibly add new curses to her ultimate curse, she starts to walk away in the direction of the bush that leads to the road that leads to the city, her gait weak but sure. Such disregard, such defiance.

As the men start discussing what to do, the interior of the hut begins to illuminate and the crackle of burning grass and poles quickly steals our attention away. The men, knowing there's nothing they can do to stop the fire, put more distance between themselves and the hut. As I move with them, I watch the woman nearing the edge of the bush. And when she disappears behind the trunk of a tree, I'm convinced she's not the type to die just because a group of wise men has said so, or because she drank her husband's dirt with a guilty verdict hanging over her, and she's definitely not the type to come back.

Those Days in April

Either you run the day or the day runs you.
Jim Rohn

Jonah had an open literature textbook in his hands. For some reason, two paragraphs caught his attention. He read them several times over, then aloud to himself: 'Who says days are the same? Who dares say they are innocent? They come – ushered in by the rising sun, kissed goodbye by the setting sun – to test us, to ascertain the stability of the ground on which we stand. They seem empty, and we think we fill them with activity – righteous or evil. In truth, they come to us replete with a measure of each of our destinies; and try as we may, what is bound to happen will happen.

'Mere spectators we stand, as our lives unfold. We heave from side to side for understanding in their brutal wake as they fade into night, only to return with a more determined aura to accomplish their purpose. No one knows exactly what they will bring. We are awestruck at their sheer majesty and oracular nature; and so we wait for the unknown. What is meant to find us will find us.' He closed the book for a moment.

The days were not ordinary in the slightest. He could feel it, let alone in the lineaments they now took on: alien, mystical. Even though it was April, when every year the farm households would celebrate harvest season with a mélange of song, dance and ululation, he felt privy to a haunting calm, like one before a storm.

In his mind's eye, he had a panoramic view of the farm, now his home for three years: to the south a borehole surrounded by three roofless walls, sty and hammer mill to the north, to the west three hills that always saw the last of the sun, five houses that formed a semicircle caught between the hills and the Great North Road, an almost-orchard of mango and guava trees between the houses and the road, and from beyond the borehole, running between houses and hills, to beyond the sty and hammer mill was a maize field that put a bounce in his grandpa's step. More than that, the farm was a place as strange as the days. Here, teenagers matured too early, missing the charm of childhood as they did. Most of his cousins were dads and moms, while others could quite easily become so. Counsel was a diamond in this environment that boasted close to fifty family members, all connected to the root that was his grandpa.

Jonah's uncles who were, like his aunts, mostly in their twenties, smoked and abused alcohol, womanised and savoured different flavours of marriage. His aunts, who like his uncles disregarded formal education, were loose with men. He had two aunts in particular, whose speciality was hopping from one truck to another at night. (The roadside was a popular truck stop.) Their conversations were centred on truck drivers and sex. The women were foul-mouthed and discussed their sexual escapades in graphic detail while making fun of the shortcomings of their men in a way no man would relish. A minute within earshot of their conversations was enough to give anyone vibrations at the meeting of the thighs.

In time, the feline grace in their movement, their heart-warming laughs, their hazel-shaped eyes, their cinnamon-coloured skin, and their hourglass figures all started to reduce to something ordinary by the day. It dawned on Jonah that the twins shared more than physical appearance and brain matter; they shared their guinea pigs, too, to a diseased conclusion.

II

'Hey! What are you doing in that tree?' Kenny said, seeming endowed with the ominous tone of the days. 'You know there're no... Oh, studying!' The expression that marked his face was of someone caught in adultery. But still, he continued, 'This studying you're now doing everywhere – at school, in the house, outside the house, in the hills, and now in trees – will make you mad!' This cousin of his was a big-mouthed, saucer-eyed hater, given to talking at the top of his lungs, seemingly having something negative to say about everything good.

Jonah, not wanting to be disturbed and without as much as a glance at Kenny, said dismissively, 'Bye.'

'You've heard me – you'll walk naked!'

'My brain is not that small.'

'So, whose brain is small? You think you're the only one who knows how to read. There're people who know how to read, real intellectuals!' Kenny said, walking energetically to cross the road into the infamous *Sodom and Gomorrah*.

A short while later, Jonah saw two of Kenny's little brothers passing by towards the main road, obviously trailing their brother. He thought they were going to get drunk. These were given to sullying him undercover. They seemed to feign indifference towards him until he heard one of them say under his breath, 'He's now a monkey,' and the other respond, 'Yeah.' They chuckled as they melted in the distance. Their brother was the lion, they were the hyenas.

No sooner had this episode passed than it struck him that he'd been gazing at the same page since Kenny's incendiary sentiments. He recalled a line from a novel: *If you can't defeat him, upset his balance*. It was as if his many cousins were privy to the line, for they knew just how to unbalance him, something that happened when an amalgam of a cavalier attitude and pure hate from this farm came to bear. It was all contrary to what he thought he merited: a modicum of understanding, support, and a few hugs if only for being double-orphaned and the only boy in his grandma's household, unlike the others where there was at least three boys – and the first wife with five. He'd got anything but.

He knew it was time to climb down. It was a cosy spot he'd found, where he could recline against one branch of the trunk and rest his feet on the one in front of him. He was surrounded by mango trees that canopied the guava tree. Together, they formed an awning over the small dirt road – the one that snaked from the farm houses to the main road. He could have sworn this configuration of trees was meant just for him.

Once on the ground, he inferred from the position of the sun that it was around 5 p.m. Darkness would not fall for about an hour. What was he to do now? An epiphany: *I could go to Nyambe's place and ask to read the book about a man who invented a machine to listen in on people's thoughts but later destroyed it after listening to his wife's and mum-in-law's thoughts. Great!*

He put his book in the house and was soon heading in the direction of those three guys, only his destination was different. His mood went from doleful to bright.

Sodom and Gomorrah was a slum. The sort of place where taverns were more popular than churches, where terms like 'drainage,' 'security,' for the larger part 'electricity,' 'good roads,' 'water reticulation,' 'education,' and 'healthcare' had no objective existence. It had a unique smell; one that reminded him of illiteracy, poverty, and neglect. And here, teenagers became parents to a standing ovation, almost.

With every step he took, he headed deeper into the bowels of this place, and the house he was going to was near the far end, nestled in the shadow of a hill. He got to Nyambe's, but he wasn't there. The small mud house that Nyambe shared with his grandma looked ignored, unkempt, uncared for. And it seemed a perfect fit in this place that was now beginning to take on the makings of isolation.

He was about to turn back when the gentle wind brought a sound to his ears. It was a blend of confounded voices, voices that were trying to grasp something otherworldly, bizarre, and ominous. On wafts of wind, he could now hear the shouting of children, the muffled shrills of women's voices and the muzzled deep tones of men. There was wonderment in the air, and he didn't know what to make of it. He willed himself to leave, but curiosity got the better of him. Soon, he had his nose in the direction of the source of the sound, his plan being to take a cursory look and leave.

The closer he got, the darker it got – until he could hardly see. But there was one place in front of him with a lot of people, and it was the only place with any sort of lighting within an approximately one-hundred metre radius. It seemed like everybody from the vicinity was there. No doubt, that was the nucleus of the uncanny brew of human sounds. *What the hell's going on there?*

Getting closer, he noticed that the psychology of the crowd was like when there's a funeral and the deceased owed the attendants hugely. In the lighting under this cover of night, he could note grimaces on people's pulled faces, they appeared distorted. Their voices, as they chatted in low tones, were equally inscrutable. It was as if everybody spoke in tongues, for he couldn't pick out anything. His heart began to throb out of tempo. Then, as though to lull him, he heard someone say to another, 'He's gone to buy a red cloth to barricade the yard.' And another, 'His disciples are already here. They're in that tent.'

In no time, he saw men clad in white long-sleeved shirts and white trousers, barefoot. He counted them; twelve in total. These were the disciples, and they were all tall and sinewy. They oozed athleticism and fitness. Even in a dream where you are a superhero, the sight of these men would make you cower.

They moved people away from the wall of the house that seemed like the subject of the gathering. A semicircle formed between the back of the house and the people. The disciples roamed the space like wolves on the prowl. One of them said, 'Wait patiently all of you! Today you'll see something you've never seen before.' His voice was powerful, authoritative. 'Our master will be here shortly. Oh! I'm sure he's back.' A sly smile punctuated his hard face.

All eyes, including Jonah's, shifted to the taxi that had just arrived. He guessed he was itching more than all gathered to see the master of these giants of men. *What kind of man is their master, and what special powers does he possess to command these men and have them revere him so?*

Then he saw an unassuming, short figure emerge from the taxi parked by the yard's entrance. The figure beckoned to the disciples; two of them approached him. He gave them long pieces of cloth that they proceeded to join together and tie around the waist-high lantana hedge that served as a fence. Whatever the red cloth symbolised now surrounded the house and the crowd of spectators.

The insufficient lighting from the lanterns could not accord Jonah any meaningful revelation of the man's features. He could tell only that he wore a black robe and his head and face were under a red hat; his feet, too, were bare. Standing away from the crowd, he cut a lonely figure. If Jonah was going to get a good look, he would have to wait for the man to get into the half-circle that was in essence a stage, where the lighting was strong.

The crowd – and it seemed like all the sons and daughters of *Sodom and Gomorrah* were here – was becoming restless, wanting to witness the spectacle. There was pushing, shoving, and grunting in the crowd with everyone wanting to get a clear view of the stage, where they knew *it* would all be happening. It grew darker the farther away one looked from the stage where six women stood with lanterns in their hands. You could feel the embrace of the starless, moonless night. An ominous hug.

The first thing the figure in black did when he came on

stage was to accentuate his space by drawing, with a long straight stick, a semi-circular line in the red ground from one corner of the house to the other. The only people he allowed in the space with him were the disciples and the six women.

He stood still, facing the crowd, his face still hard to make out under the wide-brimmed hat. 'When you see me, you see God! I have power to curse and to bless,' he said, his words measured. 'Anyone who crosses this line – this holy line – will not wake up tomorrow.' He cleared his throat. 'And call me *pastor!*'

Jonah had thought the disciple's voice was powerful and authoritative; this one was absolute power and authority. His presence was lightning and his voice thunder. The face under the hat was still hard to see, but he could tell by the roughness of his bare feet that the pastor's was a hard body. Then something stirred in Jonah's chest that caused him to want to leave, but how could he? He was on the cusp of a grand experience that he noticed was already beginning to be veiled in something Orphic – even blasphemous. His body was hypnotised and rooted.

'Time to pray! This is only for me and my disciples. The rest of you…just watch,' the pastor said, his voice sonorous.

What followed was like nothing Jonah had ever witnessed. The twelve men surrounded their master and went down each on one knee. The pastor proceeded to distribute one hard, merciless slap on each head. No sooner than the sound of the twelfth slap had died away than the six women broke into a soulful song, whose lyrics conveyed no discernible meaning. The man raised his face to the darkness above, his hat lost its hold and fell down behind him, exposing his face. It was a face similar to your imagination of a hardened criminal.

There was a hush over the crowd. The only sound was of a song, whose rhythm emanated from the deepest, well preserved parts of female souls that awaken only at the behest of a supernatural influence. It immediately became doubly sibylline when the pastor and his disciples joined in with prayers wrapped in tongues. The resultant sound was a confluence of chaos.

Jonah had always thought of himself as spiritual, not religious. As such, the goings-on made him cringe. He was leaving, his mind was made up, until he noticed that no one was moving – nothing was moving; not a soul, not the air, not even the smell of sweaty bodies. Everybody and everything was in a trance. Something outlandishly uncanny was afoot.

Suddenly as it had all begun, the prayers and the song came to a halt at the pastor's raised fists. The disciples rose, two of them rushed to the tent and came back with two sledgehammers. The pastor spread his arms, two other disciples rushed to undo his robe from behind, which fell to reveal a ripped body.

Jonah's eyes nearly left their sockets. Then he remembered something about dynamite and small packages. It was all playing out like a movie – the kind you hate but like for being different.

The crowd began to open up near one corner of the house. An old man, so ravaged by time he looked octogenarian, appeared from around the corner with a colourless plastic tub half-filled with water. Only he knew where he found the strength to carry the tub. He stopped at the line and looked around, obviously waiting for an instruction.

'Bring it here…don't be afraid, my son. I'm here to help you,' the pastor said, observing the crowd.

Jonah thought he was assessing the effect of his reference to a man old enough to be his grandpa as 'my son.' And, indeed, there was harrumphing in the crowd.

'Yes, my son, right there.' He roamed the stage for almost a minute without saying anything. Jonah guessed it was his confidence, parading his ripped self with nothing on but tight black denim shorts evidently too small to comfortably conceal the presence of a well-sized bulge at the front, that made Jonah think of a cock in a hen house.

The pastor moved to one of his disciples who handed him a bamboo stick the size of his forearms and nearly his height. He waved it in the air, satisfaction on his face as he stared at the crowd. 'I will injure you... I will kill you with this if you murmur again!' he said, his body vibrating with rage.

Jonah heard himself swallow hard. He was sure he heard a leaf hit the ground. That was the power the pastor had over this crowd; he owned it. But, his heart was hammering away at his ribcage and his throat was dry. He realised he'd been swallowing air. *No matter what, I won't give him the pleasure of owning me.*

The pastor turned to the wall and pointed at it. Before Jonah knew it, a section was being broken apart with sledgehammers. The loyal, muscular bodies were at it. The lantern-carrying women looked on with emotionless faces.

When the pastor ordered his disciples to stop, Jonah could see a bed through the hole. This had been one of the best mud houses in this place, and it appeared thoughtless to treat it so. But, like the pastor had said, he was here to help the old man – his son.

'Have you seen *it*?'

'Yes!' said the disciples.

'Catch *it* and put *it* in the water right away. *It* won't harm you. I've taken away *its* power.'

The disciples worked their way through the wall and rubble until their waists and legs were the only visible parts of their bodies.

'Ouch! Ouch! Help...*it* will kill me!' shouted one of them.

'Work together in there!'

'We've got *it*!'

'Into the water. Quickly!'

They emerged from the hole, all of them flexing their muscles trying to pacify something that only they and their master could see. The emotionless faces looked on, but it was hard to tell if they saw anything.

When the disciples finally lowered into the plastic tub the part of air they'd been wrestling with, there was the sound of embers meeting water. Then, steam trailed by the smell of fish clung to the air. The smell was strong, and everybody knew it was from that tub.

'Good job, boys. Good job!' the pastor said, dipping his left hand into the water to retrieve *it*. 'The job's done. I never fail.' He raised his hand and in it, to everybody's astonishment, was something black, dripping blood. It was the size of a grown man's hand, but it wasn't a hand – at least it didn't look like one. 'This in my hand,' he pointed at it with his right hand, 'is a hand.' He clearly revelled in the spectators' wonderment as ripples of puzzlement and praise rocked the crowd. 'This is the hand of a crocodile. It is clutching a white cloth with human blood on it and there is a needle stuck in it. Right on the side here, you can see the money note – five kwacha.'

There was suspense in the crowd as everybody waited for him to explain. He wasted no time. 'This hand was planted inside the house by an enemy, who used it to steal money and menstrual blood from female members of the family, and the needle was used to cause sickness and misfortune on the household.' He stopped and turned to his left to look at the old man who stood in the semicircle near the meeting of line and wall, looking a little shaky. 'My son, from this day onwards, this problem is gone. It will never come back. Never!'

There was applause from the gathering, with some shouting, 'Amen! Amen!' Some faces looked muted, brows creased, eyes a touch squinty, as they took it all in. Jonah's was one of those faces. He focused on the old man. *Who could have done this to the old man? Isn't it that such old people are the ones accused of doing such to others? And that old woman, the one they burnt in Kangala last month, was she innocent? But they said she was naked. Why was she naked? Anyway, it's none of my business!*

The pastor then started looking at people's palms, after which he told them things about their pasts, to which they nodded in agreement, and things about their futures, to which they reacted variously. Some were apathetic, some happy, some sad. Jonah didn't want to be part of this, so he withdrew to the back of the crowd. He was glad it had all come to an end, and he was about to leave the scene when a harrumphing boy behind him shouted, 'You're a *devil*, not a pastor! You're a *devil!*'

Jonah turned to see who had such courage, but – whoosh! – the boy bolted like a swift wind before he had the time to see and, maybe, identify him. He was left stunned, eyes wide and mouth opening and closing like a fish out of water, when the crowd made way for the pastor and some accusing fingers pointed at him. His words couldn't touch the air. Then finally he sputtered, 'It-it-is not me. He-he's-he-has run away!'

It happened so fast: Jonah was in the air and the disciples were slapping him. They kept saying, 'No one says such things to our master – *no one!*' They took him into the semicircle. The pastor approached him, a sardonic smile on his face in much the same way a predator smiles at cornered prey. Jonah had his hands at his back, unwilling to have them read if it came to that. His heart hammered away at his ribcage as if to break it. His mouth kept making soundless motions that made him feel like he was drowning. And, imaginary or not, he thought the lanterns illuminated portions of several farm faces in the crowd. *They must be having the time of their lives, itching for this moment to last forever.*

'Let me see your right hand!' the pastor said.

Jonah hesitated at this command, then a strong hand grabbed his from behind and propelled it forward where it landed in what felt to him like a pincer.

'So, you did not say that?'

'No. I did not.'

'Okay, we shall see.' The pastor opened Jonah's hand, oblivious to any resistance it offered. The crowd went completely quiet. They were all itching to learn what his tomorrow held; he could see it on their faces. Not because they cared, but because they wanted to witness a first-hand pronouncement of what great evil would befall a tiny boy who dared defame the pastor. They were hyenas watching a lion tear apart its prey.

'People bear false witness against you,' the pastor said. 'I see it in your past and in your present. And if I do nothing about it, I see it in your future. You carry a curse on your head. A great curse!' He said it so matter-of-factly that Jonah believed him. Every word was a bomb that detonated ruthlessly in his head. He hated the unsolicited attention he was getting. *Earth open up and swallow me. I want to disappear. I want to die.*

'Something is going to happen – something *big*. You see?'

Out of obedience or submission, Jonah nodded as though he saw something.

'Your friends will give false testimony against you. You'll end up in jail,' the pastor said, observing Jonah's face with the attention of a brain surgeon. 'There's hope, however. I can wash away your curse. All you need to do is bring here tomorrow, before noon, two litres of water from the river, one kg coarse salt, and one litre of milk. I'll wait for you.'

III

'So, what exactly happened?' asked his grandma. 'Why did you insult the pastor? Well, you have to do what he says – without fail.'

'I didn't insult him, grandma!' Jonah protested. He then told his grandma everything that had happened, the way he remembered it. But still, he couldn't be sure if she believed his account or that of others who got back to the farm before him. Her face reminded him of the emotionless-faced women.

He wished his grandpa were back from the city, where he'd gone to attend to his sick brother, who'd been diagnosed with meningitis at the University Teaching Hospital. He knew

– apart from believing his story – his grandpa would have given careful thought to the situation and shown him the course to take. He tried to think what his grandpa would have done in his shoes, but his brain was unhelpful.

The night was long and bereft of solace. Jonah tossed and turned, but sleep refused to embrace him. He cried his pillow wet. And when it was finally morning, he couldn't recall having slept at all.

The day appeared uglier than the previous. The smiling morning sun only served to remind Jonah of the smiling pastor. Plus, he woke to his grandma urging him to do as the pastor had instructed, even offering him K10 to buy the milk and the salt. She couldn't believe it when he turned down her offer. 'You know you have to do this. Anyway, find a way to do as you were instructed,' she said.

At least she was there; everybody else gave him a wide berth as if he had something contagious – or was it the curse? He became sure of one thing: he didn't believe in the pastor's prophecies nor was he ready to portray a wimpish character. But, he'd never been so scared!

Noon fast approached. He glanced at the sun; it seemed to be grinning. The grin turned into a smirk when he glanced at it in the late afternoon. He'd missed his appointment with the pastor, who had warned that his words would materialise in earnest if Jonah dared disobey. Immediately, a thick blanket of gloom beset every inch of his being, he felt it course through his veins like a poison. *I have to go somewhere – do something.*

He started for the hills.

Having made his way through the dry maize field, the trill of a collection of insects, the hollow – almost lifeless – song of a solitary bird, the howling wind, the choking concoction of bile and gloom, and the awareness of weightlessness at his new reality were his companions in the moment, as he ambled through the knee-high grass into the hills. The tall trees swayed in the wind, and the now red, setting sun seemed to observe him with an alien curiosity, as if to condole with him.

This surely did not have to be his fate – or did he, at any rate, deserve it? His head felt like it was taking bolts of electricity. Never before had he approached the hills, which had now become his personal sanctuary, with such trepidation. Well, there'd been a time when he'd gone to the hills to end his 'miserable' life, except he was not afraid, he was angry. But, that's another story!

His fondest memories of the hills were always of times when he would go there to read and write, and his dearest of these was when he would sit on the plateau of the highest hill, surrounded by daunting sights of tall trees and thickets, and try to be creative, writing love poems.

The painfully sharp contrast between now and then was too lucid for his sanctuary to ignore: the whole geography was resisting him, pushing him away, and distributing an immense amount of gravity where his feet fell to dissuade him from climbing. He could feel the bond he'd known to have with this place melting away, losing its hold, falling apart. He looked back at the farm, it was pushing him to the hills, and he could almost feel a whoosh of air press against his back. He knew he had to get to that almost square rock that had borne witness to his tears, anger, frustration, childishness, and genius.

Jonah couldn't remember how he'd made it to the top of the hill. But, he was there, kneeling before the rock, his whole body aquiver from sobbing. He didn't know what he was to do. Then, almost unwittingly, his lips opened, 'God, if you sent him, get me jailed, for I disobeyed him and, by extension, You. If You didn't send him, please get him jailed.'

He thought it a hare-brained thing to do as he didn't feel any divine connection, and he could count the very few times he'd said his very short prayers – two of those at his father's burial and then at his mother's three months later. Still, he felt a sense of accomplishment. His sobbing stopped.

That night his sleep was deep. Floating in a quiet, dim place where he was the only soul, a figure in a white, luminous robe appeared before him. He couldn't see its face as it had its back to him. It was hard to tell if it was near or not. It began talking to him, and then he recognised the voice. It was his father, his voice full of warmth. Jonah couldn't understand any of what his father was saying; he was speaking in tongues. He tried to share his ordeal, but his mouth wouldn't open.

When several days later the pastor's arrest on an assault charge was tom-tommed about, Jonah understood that even the bamboo stick the pastor would threaten and hit people with also had, like the days, a mission to fulfil; and that even if we don't fill the days with activity, we could, still, ever so slightly – if we persist, with a little faith – tinker with their rhythm.

Echoes of Yesterday

Time in dreams is frozen. You can never get away
from where you've been.
Margaret Atwood

I wake up with the same familiar feeling that tells me, 'Not Yet.' It has come back. And I thought it was finally confined where it belonged. When will it be over, all of it? The horror and pain of tearing flesh, the rusty smell of dried blood and of something raw and foul continue to come together and echo through my dreams from a time that refuses to remain history, whose feelers reach for me no matter how fast I run. Sometimes the haunting memory of childhood, a childhood I never knew, a brutal peeling away of innocence in a place and time of ignorance and blind passions, burns through my days and into my thoughts.

Today is different. His smile is weak, unwilling. His eyes don't sparkle and dance, and it appears to have rubbed off on the sky's eye. When he says, 'My darling,' it sounds out-of-tune. Maybe my imagination has lost the tune, but a woman just knows these things. And now that I've started to find joy in it, there was something especially cold and resigned in the way his body moved last night, like that of a man who's seen the whole picture and knows there's no hope. God knows how much I want to provide him with a target, for the man who's taught me that life can be happy deserves one; and even though he doesn't tell me, he carries himself like a man on the lip of giving up – if he hasn't already.

Mwiche and Mwiza, who were my best friends two years ago when the bells rang, avoid me like a plague, almost like I've bewitched their beloved only brother. I understand them – I tell myself I probably would be worse. They no longer visit as before and when they do, it's always official and they ensure to spend as little time as possible, like when they sometimes bring their children for weekends (they say to keep us company as, according to them, we are lonely). Well, of late, *lonely* doesn't begin to define what we're undergoing, and the presence of Lucy, Mwiche's five-year-old daughter, and Mapalo, Mwiza's six-year-old son, while a thoughtful gesture in and of itself, only serves to open the wound and exacerbate the pain.

I'm a loyal wife to my husband, and I know he's true to me. I want things to remain this way forever. But with every day that fades, I feel more untrue to him. It bothers me that he hasn't asked me about my past, for I think he needs to know that I'm the problem – the reason he keeps wasting ammunition. And because of my silence, the joy is ebbing out of our marriage and each day I see him become less of a man. It's as if I'm emasculating him, killing his manhood, especially when some of his friends who married a year ago show evidence of their nightly movements. Oh, it sucks the life out of him! But I somehow think it's enough he feels like this and I just have to find a way not to let him recede further into worthlessness, because I suspect he'll not love me the same if I tell him the truth, or his family – especially his mother – will not let him love me any more.

My heart breaks when I see him chew some roots on the advice of his friends and uncles, and sometimes drink too much milk, eat groundnuts and cheese in excess, and secretly take testosterone supplements. I want to tell him it won't work, so I keep waiting for a switch in him to flip and cause him to suspect I'm hiding something, for then he'll question me and I'll tell him everything, even if I might lose the only love I've ever known. The guilt is killing me.

Home is slowly becoming a cauldron of repressed anguish

for me and my husband. It's worse for me when his mother comes to visit as she doesn't hide that she knows I'm the one with a problem; it's in the way she talks to me, the way she looks at me, like I'm denying her the opportunity to hold what her son can produce. And I don't blame her, for a woman just knows these things. She only comes short of asking me what exactly my problem is; I don't know why but I wish she could. I'm not sure I can tell her, but it'll give me some hope that my beloved husband will one day ask, and I'll finally unburden it all and give my soul some relief.

Church is no solace either because the pastor who declared to the congregation at our wedding that we'd have many children looks at us as though we have demons or we're outside the will of God. And other church members are too polite to ask what we are doing wrong, but not Mrs Chimbipa. Last week she peeled me from the crowd after church and said, 'Agness, talk to me. Two years! Are you telling me it's family planning or what? You know, all the women here are wanting to know – they may not say it, but you know us. Your friends who only got married last year have babies. What are you two waiting for? I want you to know that you can confide in me if there's a problem.'

I wanted to tell her everything, to unload my burden. But then I remembered how my friend, Rita, ended up getting embarrassed as almost everybody got a piece of what she'd revealed to Mrs Chimbipa about her husband: that he had erectile dysfunction and relied on *Congo Dust* to perform. Even I hadn't known about this. Rita told me she'd revealed this with the view to getting a permanent solution as Mrs Chimbipa had said she could help with anything. My friend had trusted her just a little too much, and joining another church was the price she and her Elder husband paid to save the offcuts of their torn dignity.

II

My village is situated not far away from Lusaka. But growing up, it always seemed very far away perhaps because Lusaka was often hushed talk, much like it didn't belong to us. My parents told me to accept things as they were, so we were contented with our lives. In retrospect, my parents didn't need to tell me that at all as Chiuka and several other small villages and Mupata Primary School were the only places I knew on earth, my world. I loved how rich we were, how we had everything, and work was a joy. The only pain was going to school – I hated it! Perhaps it was because Falesi, Muka and I had to walk for nearly an hour and a half before we were in class. And worse, I was never good at learning, for I never grasped the importance of education when every girl I knew only went to school so she could get to Grade Seven and then be taken by a man.

My parents never explained to me why I had to go to school, so it felt like a waste of time. Sometimes the teachers would tell us education was important as it would get us good jobs in Lusaka and save us from the village. They said we should pass Grade Seven and go to secondary school, which was farther away and going there meant being prepared to walk for a little longer to and from school. I didn't need a job in Lusaka, in fact I didn't need a job at all. I was ready to live according to the way everybody lived in my village, depending on agriculture and sharing what we had. So, why would I need a job? And I definitely did not need saving from the village as it was all I knew, my all.

Every time the rough-looking, beard-keeping headmaster said we needed to succeed in our exams and go to secondary school and to university and make our villages proud, I always thought he had no respect for our way of life, like he was a traitor who was suggesting we turn our backs on the land of our birth and our traditions, and I hated him with a passion for that.

Make no mistake, headmaster Mbozi was a feared man and no one dared disobey him. You could see it in the way teachers froze at his presence and animated at his orders, he was a disciplinarian, disciplining the very teachers who disciplined us. So, headmaster Mbozi was a god in our eyes, a man whose sentiments, no matter how uncanny, always seemed to find an echo in the hearts of everyone around him. And when he bounced around the school, everyone got to work, careful to do only what was expected of them – no more, no less. When he spoke, his voice had a brutal persuasiveness that got heads nodding, bodies mobile, and hands busy. His eyes never focussed on one target for long but the fleeting moments they did focus on you, you couldn't help getting drawn into the fiery seriousness of them and you ended up praying against having them focus on you again. Such was the sheer power of personality of the man that was Mbozi.

Three months before my Grade Seven exams, my parents said I was to move to somewhere near school so I could fully concentrate on my studies and avoid missing class. My first thought was that I would really miss Falesi and Muka, but they didn't need any special arrangements as they were still in Grade Six. I told myself it wouldn't be terrible as I was going to see them in school sometimes, at least before the exam period. For sure, I was going to miss the walks and talks we'd shared. But it was necessary, said my parents, as it was going to help me prepare fully to pass my exams and make them proud. They seemed to understand the importance of education in the moment, their faces filled with a hope I only saw in them when the rains finally beat the drought. They were proud of me, and they saw something more in me – I think, potential. They knew full well my track record of bad grades, so how they expected me to jump from bottom to top of my class in three months was beyond me. They kept telling me, 'You'll pass, we know you will. You'll make us very proud.'

It was as though they were personally getting a second chance at education, to correct their own failure earlier in life, a sort of vicarious venture for them. Or, I thought, it was about competition and making a name for themselves as in the entire history of the village no one had ever made it to secondary school. And in a new twist, for whatever reason, I learned the headman had promised big to any family who would take their child to secondary school, which could well have explained my parents' new-found enthusiasm. Strangely, it seemed to give me a reason to want to succeed. So, I decided I was going to study hard and try to turn things around in the time left before exams, and just as well I wasn't going to be walking those kilometres. I was grateful to my parents for the thoughtful gesture.

Shock of all shocks was when my father said, 'You are going to stay with Mr Mbozi's family – you know, the headmaster. We just found out that we are related. In fact, he's your uncle. I went there yesterday and had a word with him. He's willing to accommodate you for the duration, and his wife, your aunt, is most welcoming. You'll have all the study materials you'll need to prepare for the exams. I'm sure you'll be well taken care of.'

Why was I even surprised that my headmaster had turned out to be my new-found uncle? It appeared everybody was related to everybody in this place, after all. Still, it hadn't occurred to me that Mr Mbozi was my uncle all those times my classmates and I would talk about him the way we did. Many people shared names, and I'd never suspected there was anything more beyond the name between my father and the headmaster. Alas, the man I'd hated with a passion was now my uncle. And it's not like I suddenly warmed to him after the revelation; I still hated him.

The Mbozi household was cordial. It was a family of four: Mr and Mrs Mbozi, the maid who came in the morning and left around sunset, and me. I learned that their three eldest children had their own homes and the youngest, a boy and a girl, were boarding in Lusaka. I found I didn't have an excuse not to study as their house had electricity, something totally alien to my village. And I remembered my mother saying, 'You'll see. Your father says they have electricity – they just turn a switch and then it becomes bright. You'll enjoy your studies better there than here where you have to breathe diesel fumes for every word you read. You'll do well, my daughter. And your father says Mr Mbozi is a very good man, a far cry from those descriptions of him you made us believe.'

My life at the Mbozi home couldn't have started better, with Mrs Mbozi turning out to be a very caring woman who spent a lot of time with me, assuring me I was going to be ready for exams and made me feel welcome, and her husband made it clear he was going to get me every necessary material to help me pass. They were so caring that, in time, our relationship began to feel very much familial. The maid, Eunice, was hardworking and kept to herself most of the time, like someone hiding deep secrets or simply afraid of getting discovered. Whatever her issues were, she didn't give me any problems and I was grateful as I needed my time to study.

I found studying could be quite a joy, a journey of discovery at every stage. I studied very hard. (Sometimes I would go back to school for prep, but I was fast getting attached to studying at home in my small bedroom.) And Eunice was a great help as I didn't have much work to do, apart from helping with dishes and a bit of cooking in the kitchen at night, after which I would again have my space.

Sometimes Mr Mbozi would bring me past exam papers and help me with Maths, Science, and English. He showed me how to answer the questions and was always ready to answer my own. And although not much improvement registered via classroom grades on tests, I felt a huge improvement within myself and I was becoming a more confident student. But somewhere in the deepest depths of me I didn't think I would be ready for exams because the more I learned, the more I saw how much I didn't know. I guess the confidence was only a result of my discovery that I could actually study and enjoy it. Still, I always remembered Mr Mbozi telling me one night, as he helped me solve maths problems, 'I'll never let you fail. You'll pass. I'll make sure of it.' He said it so matter-of-factly I thought for a moment he was going to mark my papers. His eyes appeared to be drawing me in and I found that I believed him like a father (I don't know why but I did), perhaps because he was the headmaster – he could do anything.

As more days disappeared, I found his help more useful, and he would stay up late some nights helping me with studies. He was an ideal uncle. And I discovered he laughed a lot, usually at his own bland jokes. It was hard sometimes to accept this opposite of Mr Mbozi the headmaster, who caused everybody to shake with fear in their shoes. He was transformed at home as though the veneer was lifted and the charade dropped. I recall imagining him as the lion in his household, with everybody running to do his bidding at his every roar. But not so, he was a wonderful man who wanted everybody to be comfortable in his house, and he chatted and laughed a lot with his wife. So, it confused me as to why Eunice was always aloof. Mrs Mbozi said to leave her to her unchanging mood so long she continued to do a perfect job.

One day, Mrs Mbozi went to attend a funeral of her church mate who died a mysterious death – a simple headache in the morning, death in the afternoon. She said she would come back the following morning. Mr Mbozi accompanied her, but he returned about two hours before midnight, saying he was tired and really needed to sleep. Something seemed different about him.

I stopped studying around midnight and went to bed. A few moments later, my door flew open. I opened my eyes, startled. Standing in the doorway was a different Mr Mbozi, a totally new and fierce version, naked altogether. 'Don't be afraid,' he said, as he forcefully peeled away my blanket and panties. I was in shock. My thoughts froze and I didn't know how to react. My body (and I can almost feel it even now) shook violently the whole time and whatever resistance I offered was no match for this unrecognisable creature that so easily put the headmaster in the shade. I don't know why but I couldn't scream even while he said, 'Don't worry. It may be uncomfortable the first time but I promise you, you'll learn to enjoy it, and you'll soon be begging me to do this to you every day.'

He pinned my small body to the bed, my back crashed into the mattress. He parted my legs and something hard and throbbing began to tear into me, hurting me, an extraordinary pain shot through me and went straight for my heart. I must have passed out, for I was alone in the dark when I opened my eyes. It must have been a dream, a very bad dream I had no permission to dream, but there was a trembling pain where my panties should have been. My tiny breasts felt sore, and my body was sticky all over. Dry sweat, very strong smell, not mine. To add to the sweat, my body reeked of rust and something like a weaker version of raw onion. I wanted to slide my hand to where I felt the pain breathe but decided to first try to will this into a mere dream.

When it refused to fade into a dream, I slid my right hand, whose wrist felt bruised, to the meeting of my thighs, and the pain that greeted me was like nothing I'd ever known before – it was like opening a wound. My body shuddered and I bit my lower lip so hard I thought I'd drawn blood. Then it struck me that it was real, it wasn't going away, and it was all because of Mr Mbozi.

It was as if all I had learned in my initiation ceremony culminated in this moment of pain. They'd said, 'You're now a woman. You must dance like this to please a man. Yes, like that! Very soon you'll know a man, and you must be ready.' No, I wasn't a woman, I was only a little girl. And that young, I didn't have to learn to dance for anyone, let alone be prepared for a monster who takes the virginity and innocence of a defenceless girl. I wanted to kill him, to cut *it* off.

The next day was Saturday, about a week before my exams. I pretended nothing was amiss so aunt wouldn't suspect a thing, but I was sore and I knew the cold water hadn't helped much, if at all. As I agreed with whatever she said and replied to her questions, I watched him through the corners of my eyes. He wore a smile, and sometimes the beginnings of one. He whistled, was springy, and appeared quite pleased with himself. He knew I wouldn't tell aunt because she wouldn't have completely viewed me as a victim but rather as someone who walked into her home and caused her husband to stumble, a sure way to get humiliated and hurled back to my village just before exams. I knew it would be my word against his, and, knowing him, I didn't stand a chance. So I acted as if I was fine and hoped it wouldn't repeat.

Eunice, who worked till noon on Saturdays, looked at me like she saw beyond the veneer of normality. She didn't ask me anything but her eyes were full of knowing, like she'd witnessed the whole ugly episode of last night, almost like she felt my pain and confusion. Empathy. She was a very good maid, and, according to aunt, was very chatty until early that year when she withdrew into a shell which aunt hadn't known existed. Aunt would go on and on about how an ill-prepared husband could break a girl's spirit, and she always saw Eunice as the girl whose spirit was broken. And every time I looked at Eunice, I saw a peaceful sadness, something like untapped wisdom.

Monday came like a thief; it happened upon my healing, but I was able to move without as much pain as Saturday and Sunday. I was back in class doing revision and going through passed exam papers. And so the week went.

On the Sunday night, he showed me something that looked like one of the past exam papers, only it had the next day's date on it. He said to keep it a secret between us. He showed me all the answers to the questions, promising everything would be all right if I just trusted him. We stayed up late while he gave me all the answers; we looked up answers in text books to some questions that were clearly beyond him. Every night of that week had been fun, it felt like play, more like solving a puzzle you knew you were bound to get right. And all those times he didn't appear anything like the monster that broke my body; he was helpful, sweet, and unapologetic. I yearned for him to bring up the incident but he did not, so I decided to forget it altogether – maybe I even forgave him.

He asked me to stay behind at school on the last day of exams. We talked about how easy the exams were. He assured me Grade Nine exams would be just as easy if I yielded myself to him completely. It was then he reverted to the monster and defiled me on the table in his office. My resistance didn't mean a thing and my voice couldn't come out. I closed my eyes and cried hot tears, but it felt more like bruising than tearing flesh this time, the pain was bearable. So I stayed awake behind closed eyes, drowning in the indignity of the moment. And all the while, having pinned my body to the top of the table and humping it without a shred of mercy, he kept saying, 'Don't worry. You'll learn to enjoy it. Thank me; I've made you a woman.'

I left the following day.

III

Dad said, 'Have you told anyone else?'

'Only Mum.'

'Okay, good. We should keep it this way; no one else needs to know. He's your uncle; we shall take care of this matter within the family.'

I'd expected too much of my parents; they weren't going to get him punished, they struck me as incapable of that with their casual reception of my ordeal. I'd imagined dad struggling to contain an inferno in his chest at my report and mum in hysterics, wanting the matter to be reported to the police and/or to the District Education Board. All mum kept saying was, 'Are you okay? How could such a nice man do such a horrible thing to you...how?'

Her questions irked me even more. To start, it was evident I wasn't okay, and he was definitely not a nice man, he was as horrible as his horrible act. And when the following day they went to meet with him and came back looking less than disturbed, actually calm and refreshed, I was devastated beyond words. They told me the issue had reached 'an acceptable conclusion' and it was never to be discussed again, and that it would jeopardise my chances of marriage if the village learned of it – just like that! Marriage? I wasn't interested! And in the coming few days they appeared fairly pleased with themselves and me, much like I'd achieved something big for them. Meantime, I was drowning deeper and deeper into an ocean of self-loathing and hate; self-loathing for the dirt and memory I carried, and hate for everything masculine, hate also for my parents' handling of the matter.

There were times I would jolt out of his merciless hold in the heart of night, with something breaking in my chest, panting. Then it would be as if he'd been there, the air would carry his raw onion scent, and my body would almost feel his weight. And one night I swear I felt his wide chest heave into mine and heard him breathe over my face. He was a spectre that owned my dreams and haunted me at will. He'd be smiling and laughing one moment, then grimacing and hurting me the next. Sometimes I'd see my parents cheer him on.

He had hurt me so much that I started waking up sick in the mornings, and I'd puke up something watery and bitter; it would brew, churn, then twist my insides and yank them up my alimentary canal before stopping short where gullet meets mouth, then the bitterness would shoot out with a violence potent enough to kill a cobra. Kindly, the sun seemed to take away my sickness every time it strode its first quarter across the blue canvas. Then one day mum brought home herbs: rhizomes and spiky green leaves. She boiled them and stored the decoction in a calabash. She said it was to be my *drinking water* until I was cured (and it was eye-shutting bitter that only my puke came close).

After two days on the decoction, I woke up with clots of blood in my bed and was afraid the monster had struck again. Mum said it was good as now my sickness was gone. And true to her word, I stopped observing the sun and everything was as before.

IV

'No. No! You have to proceed,' dad said, shaking his head as if to realign his brain. 'You are the first one from this village to make it to Grade Eight; and not only that, you got the best results by a girl in the whole district. No, you have to go to secondary school. You have to.'

'Yes, my daughter. Your father is right. You have made us proud, the whole village is proud of you, and the headman says he has a sweet surprise in store for us. Think about it.'

I could see desperation and disappointment begin to dominate the pride on their faces. Still, I told them I didn't want to do anything that would make me feel forever indebted to uncle; I wanted to forget him and any sort of advantage he'd offered me. I should have failed terribly had I used my own brain in the exams, I knew this, and so when everyone was celebrating my success and congratulating me, my nightmare kept recoiling back on me. I didn't want secondary school; at best, I didn't deserve it. And I was soon the villain when I put my foot down and refused to budge.

Mum said I needed to marry then, to salvage some dignity for the family, and she believed Solomon would make the best husband. There was something about marriage that made the village forget all the ill and disappointing reputations of those who were marrying; it was largely the panacea for an unwanted past and a rebirth into a dignified adult life – the most respected of all institutions.

So when Solomon's people approached, my parents were most happy to receive them. And more than anything, I did it for them and married Solomon, who was not at any rate etched in my heart. But it didn't matter because nobody looked for love, and lucky were those upon whom Cupid happened. Love and marriage: marriage was the institution and the former didn't spawn it, as we were made to believe.

As it turned out, Solomon was a good and understanding husband. He'd say, his eyes fixed on mine, 'Don't worry. Yes, people will talk, but you will be with child when the gods think it best. We have to be patient, you know.' He was my pillar in the insistent salvo of ridicule, my ray of light in the dark, and I grew to need him as much as the air I breathed. And although it felt no more than a duty, I was prepared to stick with him for a lifetime – until he buckled under the pressure after two years and took, as a second wife, my childhood friend, Alice. It was she who had told me to hold on, that I would have a child and shame all the talkers, and that the gift of the womb was a prerogative of the gods who gave as they pleased.

One year in, Alice bore Solomon a son they called Mapalo (meaning blessings). It was very much the last lap for me, I knew it. And whatever little happiness I felt for her was shrouded in shame, bitterness, and a powerful feeling of weakness. To compound my state was what I thought was Alice's new treatment of me as some sort of maid; I was happy to help, but it made me feel the way I believed Eunice felt: used. Plus, the way the village women looked at me when they came to visit her and her baby told me everything I needed to know. I would never be accepted as a woman, and it was time to leave.

I confided in mum about my plan to run away and join my aunt, her younger sister, who'd recently moved to the city with her husband.

V

Why did I marry Paul? Well, I took the chance without a second thought to spend my life with this sweet soul who has the power to heal my broken spirit and erase my past, which he refuses to dignify with an inquiry, and for the first time I know how dangerously capable of love I am, that I overlooked my childlessness with Solomon and hoped for a miracle this time.

There are things one wants to forget desperately and pretend they belong in another's past, but sometimes those demons are determined to hunt you down, even willing to enter the light to pull you back into the darkness. I've prayed for a miracle, for God to make me fruitful and wipe my tears, for a chance to live my own life and make my own mistakes. And if Paul's beatific smile should fade and his eyes dull and forget to dance, if this heaven I've found should escape me, I'll know I was loved by the best, at least before he was made to decide he wasn't. And so, echoes of yesterday put my fate beyond me.

The Business

Religion is the sigh of the oppressed creature, the heart
of a heartless world, and the soul of soulless conditions.
It is the opium of the people.
Karl Marx

The song fills the building, as the congregation joins the
Praise Team in singing.

Yahweh, Yahweh,
Yahweh, Yahweh,
Yahweh, Yahweh,
Ya-ahweh.

It feels like an invitation to a form of possession. I hear
unintelligible languages start to surge. Everyone is singing, it
appears, so I join in. I stand, hands raised and eyes half-closed,
I rock my head from side to side, my neck half-yielding. It's
as if the whole congregation is catching an unseen *wave* with
our upper body movements; this reminds me of the worship
scene at Eywa's shrine in James Cameron's *Avatar*. We sing
the song over and over; and somehow, the *wave* ends up in
my head until I begin to feel sleepy and detached from my
body. No, I don't want this; I'm only here for the money.

Mum would repeatedly say, 'Amos, you must go to church
someday, you know. Church is good for you, for all of us.
Try it one day.' And I'm here in Matero this Sunday morning
getting an experience of church. I knew when I told her I was
going to visit my friend, Ben, in Matero I was actually heading
to Miracle on Miracle Ministries headed by the domineering
prophet famously known as 'Commando-1.' If I see Ben today,
it'll be after I've got my money quadrupled.

II

A year since I graduated from the Copperbelt University with a bachelor's degree in Chemical Engineering, no promise of a job on the horizon as companies are trimming their workforces owing to the underperforming economy and an ever-rising cost of doing business. Lusaka is not a kind place – and one has to be sharp. So, seeing mum struggle to fend for me and my three little sisters, who are still in school, I decided to start a business to help out at home; I could help with the rent, for instance. But owing to the beat-down economy, people now tend to hold on to their money and start-ups fail. And business ideas themselves have been hard to come by after seeing friends fail time and again: Hamududu lost his money in that second-hand shoe business, Mumbi and Soki put money together and saw their restaurant business eat it, and Naomi's salon business went down the drain. It's as if people have decided to stop wearing shoes, eating, and getting their hair done. Bleak picture. The truth is that the only businesses with any sort of life are the veterans whose taproots have sunk deep into the little moisture that remains, but even they are struggling; and to keep afloat, they are laying off most of their workers.

Knowing that mum had been willing to lend me a small capital to start something of my own, I finally had a business idea after watching Commando-1 on ZNBC TV last Sunday. I haven't shared it with anyone because, I must confess, it feels a little dishonest. I don't think it is, though, as it happens in what has come to be considered as the holiest of all churches in Lusaka: Commando-1's Miracle on Miracle Ministries. He has said it long enough: 'God dwells here. God resides here with me,' and now they believe him. Maybe I believe him, too. They come from the ends of the country: Livingstone, Chipata, Luapula, Mwinilunga, Mongu, Solwezi, and places in-between to receive their miracles at the hands of the revered *commando* of God. He says there's nothing impossible with him, and no one can argue the contrary. He's the epitome of the modern prophet, the one who hears directly from God and gets fresh revelations that put the Bible in the shade and make it appear almost obsolete.

I watched as money quadrupled. It was Commando-1 operating in the beyond-and-above, kicking demons that way, ailments this way, curses and bad luck that way, and bringing, in his own words, 'heaven down to earth,' after which he asked the congregants to check their pockets, purses, wallets, and bank accounts. (He didn't mention money in the build-up to this.) And one by one, they started heading to the pulpit as though driven, wonder plastered their countenances as they peered into their phone screens and purses and wallets, while some men dipped into their pockets and counted money. He stood there in the pulpit looking majestic, smiling that big smile of his that rivals your image of the smiling God. The ushers, in a manner that seemed well rehearsed, moved the microphones to the wowed congregants, and all of them who got a chance to speak said their money had quadrupled under the anointing of the prophet.

He said, 'There's a reason why I have this great anointing. God saw fit to give me an anointing greater than the one He placed on Jesus, so that I perform greater works. And even Jesus knew there would be one greater in deeds. You have seen nothing yet! In these end times, great and greater miracles, unprecedented miracles will be performed in this church, and happy are you who have chosen to belong here. There will be more healing and more money; you will receive miracles according to your faith, and money according to your money.'

My plan was born, and I knew I would be in Matero today.

I asked mum for the capital she'd promised to give me. I refused to tell her what business I was contemplating. She said, 'Amos, be serious. Don't lose the money. But if, like you've promised, you will give it back, no problem.'

I ended up with K1000. I didn't have a pair of trousers with many pockets, so I went to *salaula* and bought myself khaki cargo pants. Pockets on the back, the front, and the sides all the way to the bottoms. Perfect. This way I could divide the remaining K950 into small denominations for each of the twelve pockets. I imagined myself leaving Miracle on Miracle with quite a haul.

III

The repetitive, unintelligible languages take over, as I see ordinary people transform into unrecognisable beings. Some intersperse their transfiguration with queer laughter, some with jumping and shaking as though conducting electricity, and some with total blankness before they go back to their eccentricities.

There's a big screen behind the prophet depicting an outside, under-the-marquee version of the goings-on: people jumping, shouting, screaming, while some are in wheelchairs and on stretchers, looking utterly desperate. And uncanny as I find this place, everybody is a part of the disorder and noise except – as far as I can see – me, the prophet, the guy playing the keyboard, the cameramen, and the ushers walking the aisles and peddling holy water and anointing oil on trays in much the same fashion as street hawkers do, with Commando-1's face frozen in a smile on the 50ml bottles.

It's an enormous building of high white walls that, according to TV, has a 12,000 seating capacity (if I recall the figure correctly). Being here today, I feel the sheer size of this place, and to think there's another gathering outside. I'm in one of the middle pews near the front, seated next to a thin bespectacled female congregant. The two very long aisles each have a huge pillar supporting the building midway from the pulpit and the back; both disappear into a white ceiling that beams with bright lights through its glass sections – it reminds me of the most beautiful firmament, one I saw in my childhood.

The prophet stands in a waist-high pulpit, the Praise Team section to his left. There's a well-carpeted space between the pulpit and the first row of pews, which I remember the prophet used for healings when I saw him on TV last Sunday.

Through my half-closed eyes, I see everything and, not for the first time, I feel like both a rebel and a spy. I see tears; the thin woman beside me, her face is wet, as are several others. I wonder what's making them cry, what problems they grapple with, how heavy their burdens must be.

Strange as it may sound, I find myself entertained and my mind shifts from wanting this episode to end to wanting it to continue. And why are females visibly more connected to the *wave*'s charge than all the males I see? For it is the women who are making the most noise and throwing themselves to the white-tiled floor, unmindful of what parts of themselves they reveal as they do. I'm beginning to see too much.

The sound of the keyboard rips through the noise and brings me back to church. The song comes alive again and, like it all started, the edge disappears off the antics and unknown languages, and a calm begins to settle. I see open eyes, so I completely open mine. Hankies come out and go to work on faces. Tops and skirts, and dresses fall back onto bodies. The thin woman's face is dry and beams a bright smile; it's hard to believe she was in tears and broken-looking a moment ago. She looks at me and her eyes dance behind the glasses. The people I'm looking at now appear better than before the *wave*; they seem fulfilled, relaxed, and ready.

'Come to me all ye who are heavy laden and I will give you rest,' he says.

I remember seeing those words emblazoned in red on that huge, white church banner under the name of the church in black. Oh, people carry burdens untold! And it appears that to say such is to invite all of Lusaka, the whole country.

His voice repeats the words deeply, slowly. He is imposing, like someone high on something as he struts about the pulpit in his full, white gown.

His dress code has clearly struck a chord with some of his loyal congregants as I see several men in full-length, long-sleeved white robes and brown sandals, making them look pure-hearted and celestial but none to the degree of their avant-garde prophet, who carries an aura of realms beyond and above mankind, reality, and the times.

When he says those words, it's not like he's referring to anything or anyone other than himself (intended or not, it's hard to tell). But he sure has the stature to say he was in heaven last night, and no one would find it in themselves to express the slightest doubt. I'm cocksure that the same way I have conversations with my family, he has his with God and angels anytime. And he looks like an angel. I've never seen one in person before, but he looks like one of those drawings of angels in books – except black.

'Just as it is every Sunday, it shall be unto you according to thy faith.'

Faith. Was it why some people remained stuck in their pews when others were charging forward last week? No worries, mine is overflowing – and specific. It made me ask for capital, spend five percent of it on pockets, and *sow a seed* of K200. He said to sow a seed and expect a harvest, and that you don't reap where you don't sow.

'It is the difference between those who receive and those who don't. The Spirit is telling me He wants to go a step further today. Yes Holy Spirit, I'm listening.' He's quiet and calm, looking like a beautiful statue. He's receiving his orders and revelations for the service. There's a soul-piercing silence, except for the tune that speaks of a supernatural quality, a prelude to something miraculous, divine.

Two to three minutes elapse before the statue becomes animate; it happens every Sunday. Commando-1 is ready. It's time!

He raises his hands and some of the white separates from above him – it's a dove. It hovers over the pulpit to the utter astonishment of the congregation. His eyes are willing it to settle on him, but it doesn't have to as most of these people are already on their knees sputtering, 'J-J-Jesus. J-Jesus,' as it flies over the congregation to the back of the church and back to the pulpit before it goes to catch some rays out through the door to the right of the prophet. On the huge screens behind him, one by one, giants stand up from their wheelchairs and those on stretchers start to sit up, as praise fills the marquee.

New tears.

'You haven't seen anything yet. Please get back to your seats. He wants to save you from the world, from those who say they have solutions but only want your money. How much money have you wasted on fruitless ventures? Remember, you reap a hundredfold when you give to Him,' he says, pointing to the roof (or beyond it).

A hundredfold? My harvest? Today? My heart begins to race for joy.

'There are people here who have fallen victim to witchdoctors or *professors* – whatever they call themselves now – who post adverts on every street light promising all manner of interventions from breast, hip, and penis enlargement to riches, to bringing back lost lovers, to winning court cases, to passing job interviews, and to every other thing they cannot do. The devil is a copycat; he's a liar, a giver of counterfeit things.

'You are in the right place, for here you get no counterfeit; and I've said and proven it time and again that there's nothing impossible in this environment of anointing. I'm here to fight and win battles for God; I'm his anointed *commando*, and I'm here to prove to you that you don't need those witchdoctors. That's why I'll give you a modicum of the miraculous today, with more to come in the near future.'

The excitement is infectious, faces ooze with expectation and something more. Catharsis. I wonder which of those promises he's going to manifest today. I hope it's riches. If not, I'll very much welcome enlargement; yes, enlargement – so long it happens in my pockets.

Everybody is expectant.

'It's God's plan to focus on one important issue today. And I must emphasise that you catch your miracle when it shows up, as in the case of these special miracles. I rarely repeat special miracles and I never repeat most of them, so catch them while you can. Remember, your faith is the key. Today's special miracle is enlargement...enlargement for men...penis enlargement.'

Commando-1 lays hands on about two dozen men who have walked into the miracle area. Screens beam him live. He says, 'Holy Spirit, enlarge his territory, enlarge his *territory*,' as he pushes each man's head backwards. The ushers catch the falling bodies and lay them down on the carpet. In no time, the carpet is enduring the weight of the sprawling men. The screens zoom in on their faces. Some of them, as I see now, are barely men, teen-looking.

'Move in a special way and perform operations on each man's *member*. They have refused to embrace shame and spurn this opportunity. Therefore, dear God, enlarge their *territories* according to your will, and take away their shame. Let them find the joy of manhood in your presence henceforth. Why should men have tools of children? How will they, then, please their women? Reward them a hundredfold for their courage and willingness to catch this miracle. In the name of Jesus!'

The semi-conscious faces start to leave the screens, to be replaced by a close-up of a heaving white shirt with shiny silver buttons running to a black belt's buckle, then to the fly of brown trousers now displaying evidence of what just happened; it seems to conceal something the size of a big fist breathing pugnaciously, rhythmically to the *Amens*, *Hallelujahs*, *Praise Gods*, and *Glories* of the congregation, and the thin woman, as though unaware of herself, stands up and punches the air above her *Brazilian* head, shouting, 'Commando-1, give us more!'

Commando-1 says, 'Dear God, thank you for manifesting your power. I ask that you give these men the total package so that they fall not prey to shamans and all other imposters out there. To their enlarged *territories*, add power – power to hold up their miracle. Remove all weakness in that area and give them power! Power! Power! Power!'

The congregation attacks the air, responding, 'Power!' while the thin woman shouts, 'Yes, more power!'

IV

One by one the men stand up, clutching at their groins, each of them carrying blank facial expressions laced with something between satisfaction and bewilderment – resignation almost.

A smiling female usher, whose appearance screams teenager, asks, 'Tell us, have you received your miracle?'

Commando-1 looks on, smiling light at the congregation. And just before the men start to testify, a fluttering of wings is heard above them and – behold! – two white doves circle the pulpit before, in unison, they fly out into the sun. The congregation is in excited disorder. Gratification begins to edge confusion off the faces of the men; and the longer the excitement lasts, the more assured they look, and it's their faces that now fill the screens. I observe all this with the eye of someone who's going to write about it.

The female usher repeats the question, and the prophet repeats the smile.

The owner of the brown fly, who seems to have no idea that his *territory* was the subject of national TV a moment ago, says, 'I want to thank God for using Commando-1 to move in mysterious ways. I'm speechless, really speechless. Commando-1, may you continue to show the power of God in ways unheard of. Until now, I suffered quietly like most men, carrying a shame whose brunt my wife bore, a shame unknown to others but eating me slowly inside, emasculating my manhood. I'm more than grateful to you, Commando-1. And always know that in me, you have a loyal servant who will sow in the ministry to the full extent of sowing. Thank you for lifting my shame. Thank you Jesus!'

Focus shifts to a woman whose smiling face fills the screens, and it seems a little more pleased than the thin woman's.

The usher asks the men a variety of questions, all drilling down to the miracle and how it has made them feel. They all, in essence, say similar things.

'Thanks Commando-1.'

'Thanks God.'

'Thanks Jesus.'

'Do more.'

'I'm your loyal servant.'

'I'll sow in the ministry.'

Commando-1 is back in the pulpit and it's his face on the screens. He says, 'Sow your seed in fertile ground. Blessed are you who sow in this ministry. The more you sow, the more you reap – it's a principle. Come for more miracles next Sunday, all ye who are heavy laden, and I will give you rest.

'Before you leave, remember to buy water, oil, lotion, brooms, stickers, hankies and *chitenges* while stocks last – oh, yes, and caps. Remember we now have caps for young ones too. See any of our lovely ushers on your way out. And I must mention that next Sunday we shall have sandals on sale for all those who want to bless the ground on which they walk, to nullify charms put in their way and automatically send them back to the sender. Oh, be sure to get those sandals!'

'Yes Commando-1!'

'Yes papa!'

'Glory!'

'Tell us prophet! Tell us!'

V

The sun throbs in the sky between two white feathers of cloud. I raise my face and look at it from behind my eyelids, as flames of red and deep-orange dance in my face. The warm sun is real, so are the clouds, this I know. But, are the flames real or merely a figment of my imagination?

It shouldn't feel like such a long walk to the bus stop, next to the famous Musadabwe Bar. I walk on, only minimally aware of my surroundings, feeling like I just lost my life's earnings on gambling, like the biggest idiot on earth. And what sort of story shall I tell mum? I feel my every conviction drain out of my being, leaving me dry and at the mercy of the sun.

Life

I am learning to love the sound of my feet walking
away from things not meant for me.
AdventureDaze.com

You didn't know much about paintings but, weirdly, your
mum's slim face fascinated you. You looked at it like it
were the Mona Lisa, like you were trying to piece together
the story behind it, and yet, even more weirdly, you saw
something ebb from it, from its eyes, from its smile every time
a man walked out of her life.

And, you wondered if something left your face when,
in your bedroom some nights, that image, that elusive face
flirted with the space between awake and asleep, that face
of a man whose features refused to come together – you
knew it was a man because, in the collage, there was also a
moustache, strong jaw and angry eyes. You wondered, too,
if every next morning your mum would drive you to school
your face turned flaccid. It was probably a residual image of
some powerful presence in your past, you told her. It was just
the beginning of your dreams, she'd say. She'd respond to
you the same every time you brought it up. But something
left her every time, something like moisture, and it made you
suspect she'd rustle if you clasped any part of her body, just
like a dry leaf would.

II

Chongo wasn't the first nor was he to be the last. He came
into your mum's life like sunshine, and into yours like a sort

of storm for the gentle violence of an uninvited convenience with which he came. He was a drizzle at the start, then a downpour as the months wore on. In all this, your mum seemed to shine, almost like she'd been a diamond in the dirt before he showed up. But what was it to matter to you for as long as you saw the moisture return to her face? It was all you ever wanted, her happiness, as you found it did something wonderful to your confidence. Gone were the days when she'd come to pick you up from school bored and listless, slumped in the driver's seat, listening to Tony Braxton's 'Unbreak My Heart.' You'd beg her to stop playing the song, to which she'd say she played it for the tune – not the lyrics. Other cars would leave the car park of your school and smiles from your friends and their parents would flash from behind the windows and you'd wonder what songs were playing in their cars, what conversations they were having.

Chongo was a game changer; even the air in the house became light, and dinner times became happy moments when you would all chat and laugh between mouthfuls. He'd share his childhood experiences, most of them funny, some you found plain disgusting. 'My dad was always clean-shaven,' he said. 'One day his elder brother, my uncle, from the village came to visit. During lunch – and we always ate as a family – I pulled hard on his beard that seemed like it'd never met a blade. He uttered yelps. All eyes on me, I said I wanted to remove the wig because it made him look ugly; I pointed to his bald head and suggested he put it there.'

You found this part particularly funny.

'That night at supper,' he continued, 'my uncle told me secretly not to eat some of the fruit salad as the yoghurt was actually an old woman's puke.'

You were eating your fruit salad when he told this part. You felt your stomach protest, almost churning the food back up. Not a pretender, you gave him the look, not quite the look you gave Mr Thompson when he suggested you couldn't have written that essay by yourself, but quite the same look you gave the waiter at the school canteen when you found a cockroach in your lasagne. Ugh! And all your mum did was look away.

You started it. Yes you did, then your mum followed cue. But negotiating for a dinner at his place felt like the USA trying to strike a nuclear deal with Iran and North Korea in tandem or like trying to get Putin to bow to the US presidency. At least Mr Thompson had made clear to you the impossibility of success in those two scenarios. If your house was in New Kasama and his in Chalala where he lived with his sister, you thought going to his place for dinner, even once, shouldn't be an issue.

The first time, he took your mum to My Asia at Manda Hill. They watched a film afterwards at Sterkinekor, and he brought her back around midnight. The next time, you accompanied them to Mike's Kitchen at Arcades. Both times he gave the excuse his sister wasn't home to help cook dinner. Promising *next week*, he was out of excuses, but his next week didn't come. Still, your mum indulged him, and like most things ignored, eventually the talk of dinner at his place became a nebulous memory.

Your mum became cosier with the man she'd asked you to call *uncle* – just before she convinced you to call him *dad* and he started spending weekends with her, in her bedroom, while you tried to piece the collage together. You started to feel uneasy about things, in utter contrast to her ebullient manner. So when on that morning, her spirits soaring as she started the car, Osvaldo, the guard, opened the gate and the front of the car just started to kiss the tarmac, a heavyset woman, chest heaving, stopped the car and started shouting obscenities at your mum, you weren't as surprised as she was – she was petrified. She rolled down her window. The woman's mouth kept opening; you didn't see it close once. 'If you're a woman – a real woman – come out, let's end it right here. For months my husband is not the man he used to be; you've bewitched him. Who are you? Tell me, who are you?!

Why can't you find your own?! Are you so ugly that you can't find your own man? Chongo is my husband of five years. We have two sons together. You home-wrecker...'

It was the way the car had taken off, leaving the woman still standing, hurling expletives as if the stone she'd thrown at the boot hadn't done enough damage, that unsettled you even more. Had your mum known? She never shared with you the details of her affair with the man you knew you'd not be calling *dad* again.

She drove like it was a punishment, but more than this it was her subdued silence that made you feel for her. She even forgot to play some music in the car, so unlike her. And since she seemed to need the quiet, if it brought her any peace or clarity of thought, you decided to ensure your thoughts didn't become words.

After you'd got out of the car in the school's drop-off area, she forgot to say something to you when she restarted the engine. But you let it be, the elephant was getting fatter and fatter between the both of you. You watched the car leave in the most unsteady fashion you'd ever seen – wobbly as a learner driver's car, the hum of the engine like an apology.

As you walked to class, it tore at your heart why your mum hadn't said a word to the woman. Now the haze started to lift over whether she'd known about the other woman; you thought she hadn't. But what did it matter seeing she hadn't said something when she should have? She should've said something even just to wipe the grin off Osvaldo's face. Yes, you'd seen it in the rear-view mirror; you also saw the curious surprise on Emelia's face, as she arrived to start her work day. You felt something leave your face at the thought of the guard and the maid tearing into the topic and probably sharing it with other guards and maids. The shame.

The hours flew by. Mr Thompson, Madam Cordelia, Mrs Smith, Monsieur André, Madam Bertha, and then Senhor Moutinho, the new English Literature teacher, an unassuming Portuguese man with what you thought was an overly friendly air. You itched to learn if he'd be as lacklustre as his predecessor, Mr Lee, who taught like he was teaching his grandma or putting babies to sleep, like he was drifting into sleep himself.

If the new teacher thought anything of you, you thought he thought you detached and conceited as everybody else clamoured for his attention, participating in every way possible. They answered and asked questions. Many misplaced answers and questions.

'Charles Dickens wrote Macbeth.'

'No. He wrote The Two Cities – A Tale of Two Cities.'

'How did you end up studying English Lit in Portugal? Does it mean you don't have something called, say, Portuguese Lit in Portugal?'

'We do have Portuguese Lit and we're very proud of it. We do have literature greats in Portuguese Lit the same way English Lit has its greats. For instance, you have William Shakespeare and we have Luis de Camões. I was born in Lisbon, grew up in London and studied English Lit before I went back home to study Portuguese Lit.'

You liked English Lit, but you found that you enjoyed African Lit more. It felt like poetry to your soul every time Madam Cordelia would mention among others Wole Soyinka, Chinua Achebe, Ngugi wa Thong'o, Nadine Gordimer, Chimamanda Ngozi Adichie, Ayi Kwei Armah, Mariama Bâ, Alain Mabanckou, J.M. Coetzee, Ben Okri, Yewande Omotoso, and Sefi Atta. Incidentally, in your heart, it felt false when Senhor Moutinho said *you* had William Shakespeare, but it rang true when he said he had Luis de Camões. Not that you knew of the author but because his name sounded Portuguese.

After class, you stood looking at your wristwatch like it was a source of repulsion, all the while your friends waved at you and you waved back, your right hand growing in weight with every raise. She showed up thirty minutes late, the car humming a gripe in its approach and appearing like it was being pushed. You decided to contain your fire. She didn't even apologise for her lateness; you wondered if she knew she was late, but you kept it to yourself. She was expressionless, inscrutable when she said *hi* and asked about your day. You told her about your new teacher from Portugal.

'Is he white?'

'Yes.'

The drive was dead quiet if not boring, save for the quiet lullaby of the air-conditioning. Her profile, you could have drawn it; it looked parched. In that moment, you gained a rough idea of just how much moisture had left her face from the time she left you at school and you were grateful you hadn't unleashed your fire at her. It would've certainly exacerbated the cracks in her profile, your painting.

Osvaldo opened the gate at the first hoot, appearing obsequious. You knew he was itching for Kambenge's shift to come so he could tell all; you saw it in his manner. But, what did it matter? It was probably such miscarriages of social order that added spice to his inert life. And what spice it was going to be to Kambenge's life!

Emelia's manner was a replica of Osvaldo's when she welcomed you home and started for the door to leave. You realised that it probably pleased people like Emelia and the guards when something happened to cause something to leave your faces. You also thought life would be very unkind to them if you didn't take care of them the way you did. You kept these things to yourself.

The sun set and soon it was time for dinner. Mashed potatoes, grilled chicken, and a lettuce salad with light Italian dressing – simple and delectable as only your mum would have it. You sat to enjoy the meal. With every chew, you grew determined to ask her some questions about Chongo and his wife. No sooner had you cleared your throat after chewing and swallowing a very tasty chunk than the both of you stiffened and your eyes rolled – the gate was opening. Perhaps your mum should've warned the guards not to allow Chongo to enter. So, like you'd grown used to, Chongo's car drove in. Next, he was knocking on the door. For a moment, it felt like the old times, like your mum would open the door, hug him and lead him to the table, to his spot, the chair that you both kept looking at as if it were a vestige of his, something unwanted.

His knees on the floor, he looked insincere. But when his words started to pour out, they sounded sincere enough. 'I'm so sorry; I never meant for you to find out that way, but my wife and I are on separation, and we have been for all the time that you and I have been together. I'm divorcing her. I want you, baby. My love for you will not allow me to live without you. I need you. I want you to be my wife. Please understand.'

But when your mum responded, it was with ice-cold authority, like that of a woman who'd tasted the ultimate disappointment and learned to live with it. 'I will not take pride in hammering out my happiness on the anvil of a man just because he's a man. I'm done with you. Get off your knees, go back to your wife and never return. For as long as I live, I don't want to see your face again.'

You knew what you'd wanted to know, and you were proud of her that she wasn't like most women. She was your mum. You went to bed with a sense of worth washing over you, especially when you recalled how her face had looked less and less parched, as she towered over Chongo, saying those words that must have pulled at, and hurt, his heart, and how every crack in her face had started to fade.

The next night saw a kerfuffle at the gate, like a small riot: a beam of light, an angry car engine, whacks on the gate, two irate voices arguing loudly, followed by prolonged hooting. You both knew who it was, but that chapter, like the gate, was never to be reopened. And you were ever so proud of your mum.

The fulfilment that attended your subsequent days was evident, you saw it on her face too. It touched every facet of your lives; it was as though your hearts hugged every time you talked with your mum, as though the car had found new life, as though school was especially meant for you, and you stopped focusing on how happy others were. Also, you came to love English Lit nearly as much as African Lit mainly for the way Senhor Moutinho taught it; he was totally incandescent about it, this touched a part of you that Mr Lee's teaching couldn't, and you saw a similar sort of passion strike a chord with other students.

Senhor Moutinho quickly established himself as a confidant and father figure to your class. Many of your classmates took counsel from him on teenage issues. He was really a caring man. He was the only teacher to notice you squint whenever you focused on something written on the whiteboard. He was the first to suggest you needed to visit an optician. 'No one has eye issues in my family,' you said. But your family was really only you and your mum. Besides, you didn't want to go to an optician and wind up with an eye disorder. Specs? Not for you.

Persistent as equatorial rain he was, so you decided to let him talk it over with your mum and gave him her cellphone number. A week later, she didn't seem surprised at all that you'd never complained about your eyes but you returned from the optician's with a pair of specs. Short-sighted.

He was one of the first people to notice you had specs on. 'Congratulations! They look good on you.'

'Many thanks, Senhor Moutinho.' No, you were more interested in whether you looked good in them.

'You look like the younger version of our family doctor,' said Ruth. Her words danced in your soul like music, because that morning the mirror had shown you something that you thought came a little close to a toon.

Aside from that, he made you think more seriously about your future and what sort of indelible mark you wanted to leave behind. He didn't just teach literature, he taught life, always finding a way to bring themes to life with real-life examples. Every new thing you learned, no matter how infinitesimal, you told your mum. Then you noticed that the very few times you'd forget to update her she'd ask. But, yes, perhaps she found your fascination with Senhor Moutinho fascinating. After all, it was because of him that she couldn't remember when last she'd reminded you to study or do your homework, and because of him you'd made the jump from your usual third position to first at the end of the second term. Your mum was ecstatic.

While he explained your report card to her, you had a soupçon of suspicion they weren't meeting for the first time. It was like that thing Senhor Moutinho liked saying about old souls, that they connected seamlessly when they met again in other lives, that they felt at home in each other's aura; it seemed to be playing out right before your eyes. Not since the height of her affair with Chongo had you seen that amount of moisture come into her face or that smile shine so. Perhaps it was his friendliness. Perhaps it was all because of your performance in English Lit.

For first term holidays, he went to either London or Lisbon – you didn't know where. For term two holidays, he should've gone to either to visit his family but he did no such thing. Instead, his 'old souls thing' with your mum took a new turn. Since he hadn't much going on during the school holidays, he came to dinner every other night, and you came to learn he was a very good cook. In time, he introduced you both to some Portuguese dishes such as Bacalhau Portuguese ao Forno, Arroz de Braga, Portuguese Shrimp, Portuguese Kale Soup, and Portuguese Beef Stew, which you and your mum found absolutely delicious.

You learned he was also a New Kasama resident – how coincidental! And by the end of the school holidays, dinner venues oscillated between your house and his. You thought it all just felt right, like a family, a complete family; it didn't feel like an experiment. The coming together felt like it'd happened before in another place, in another life, before some sort of disruption had sent it into oblivion. You found yourself fitting comfortably into the expanded aura, and all your protests began to wane. 'No mum, I hope this isn't what I think it is; he's my teacher for Pete's sake!'

Unlike you who showed no interest, your mum's was enough for him to start teaching her some Portuguese words and phrases after seeing she'd grasped the Portuguese alphabet. 'It's a very simple language if you pay attention. We shall start verb conjugations after this. Before you know it, you'll start constructing your own sentences and you can come with me to Portugal. Obrigada if speaker is female, obrigado if male (Thank you). Como vai? (How's it going?). Vai bem (Going well). A minha casa (My house). O meu banco (My bank).' It would go on and on. You ended up learning the basics, too, and your interest in the language activated.

Then one day you heard him talk about Luis de Camões. 'He is the Portuguese Shakespeare, the same way Shakespeare is the English de Camões. His poetry speaks to the soul.' He then focused his eyes on your mum's face. 'Amor é um fogo que arde sem se ver; é ferida que doi, e não se sente; é um contentamento descontente; é dor que desatina sem doer.' It was enough to get you to join the class.

When the third school term came, you found yourself looking forward to weekends, to leaving class things behind and getting together as family; and this time, except for Fridays when you'd meet for dinner only, Saturdays and Sundays were for lunch also. You spent more and more time together at weekends and you liked even more what it did to your mum's face. Around midterm, aside from spending every weekend at your house, Senhor Moutinho started sleeping in your mum's bedroom. She said you had to take him as your father. 'He'll officially move in with us early next year,' she said. But you found it difficult to call him *dad* because he was your teacher before anything else, so you addressed him simply as *Senhor*. It didn't matter, you felt, so long as you called him *dad* in your heart every split second before *Senhor*. You didn't want to force it; you believed it was going to come as naturally as sunrise, and they both understood.

You couldn't ask – though you itched to know – the shape and tone of conversations between the guards and the maid. Did their conversations carry some form of dignity for your mum, or did they expect to see another woman – a white one this time – storm your house and hurl vulgarities at your mum? You knew one thing, regardless: they looked thirsty for spice and they'd gone back to seeming like some unknown entities were living their lives for them, present but absent.

Your school's academic year came to a close at the end of November. On the Thursday of that final week, parents came to meet with teachers, to collect report cards and discuss how well or badly their children had performed in the exams. Your mum didn't show, and you hadn't expected her to as your *dad*, being your class teacher, was going to bring your results home at the weekend. Moreover, you and your friends already knew from the marked scripts that you'd scooped first position – again.

The following day, your school had an end-of-year party in the school hall. Parents had been invited to attend and savour their children's performances ranging from song and dance, poetry, drama, to gymnastics, interspersed with speeches from your principal and other management officials. There was also a category where three teachers' names were mentioned, and the student vote gave Senhor Moutinho first place as The Most Inspiring Teacher; his runners-up were Madam Cordelia of African Lit and Mrs Burke, a teacher of Global Perspectives. A good number of your classmates punched the air and shouted congratulations when his and Madam Cordelia's names were called. The joy on Senhor Moutinho's face complemented that in your heart and on your mum's face. She sat there flashing a big radiant smile, only stopping short of leaping for joy. But when you performed Ben Okri's 'As Clouds Pass Above Our Heads,' adroitly bringing it into tune with Secret Garden's 'Pastorale,' she was the first to stand at the end and applaud, while her eyes, and those of many others, filled with tears.

'Astonishing – the way you gave it life,' she said later.

Having decided he'd only go to Portugal on December 28th, for the last two weeks of his holidays, that meant you were to have him around for the next four weeks, in which time he moved permanently to your house. You guessed they couldn't wait for next year, and the only thing missing was a wedding ceremony. One day, as the two of them chatted, you heard her mention Civic Centre, to which he nodded the same way you did whenever you got an epiphany.

III

He suggested flying Mahogany Air, but she thought the drive would be more fun than shooting through the air and landing in Livingstone in an hour. 'We'll also have the advantage of driving to any place we want without having to make arrangements with tour operators,' she said. Her idea of fun appealed to you. You imagined the three of you in her latest Toyota Land Cruiser Prado going from Lusaka, through Kafue, Mazabuka, Monze, Kalomo, Zimba, all the way to Livingstone. You could feel the thrill in your heart.

With her in the driver's seat, having given Emelia a week off, you left Lusaka with the rising sun on the 20th and arrived in Livingstone around 1 p.m. The ride had been exhilarating, and he was grateful for it as he'd seen the towns on the way he wouldn't have seen had his Mahogany Air idea materialised.

You spent the rest of the day at the David Livingstone Lodge and Spa on the banks of the Zambezi River. It was great when you sat on the deck; it gave you the feeling of floating, with the river twirling and washing against the support pillars under you. You felt so in tune with nature.

Night came. The three of you chose a table near the balustrade, it made you feel closer to the river. For supper, your mum selected fried Zambezi bream, chips and a salad for everyone. After the meal, you drank your orange juice while they drank Pina Colada. There was no mistaking it all the while, just how happy they were, how much of a loving family you'd become. If you ever fell in love, you wanted to be as happy as they were, chatting and laughing like children, a touch of a smile always on their lips, their eyes beaming whenever they looked at each other. Sometimes you thought they'd forget you were there, like the way their meeting of lips would sometimes, without warning, turn into full-on kissing only to stop abruptly because you cleared your throat. So you learned to excuse yourself whenever you noticed the heat rise between them.

You retired to your room and they to theirs. You spent some time looking out of your window at the activity on the deck and on the river, people eating, people drinking, people chatting, people observing the arrival of the tour boats that you were looking at, people disembarking and chatting noisily, some singing out-of-key songs only they knew, looking possibly much happier than before the cruises, like some wonderful magic had happened to them. Your head on the pillow, like many nights since Senhor Moutinho came into your and your mum's life, you didn't see a moustache, nor a jaw, nor angry eyes, and your sleep was deep and restful.

After breakfast the following day, you left for the Victoria Falls. The Knife-Edge Bridge was fun, with the white sheet of falling water hitting the rocks and spraying back far above the top fold of the sheet and the bridge and falling as rain. The sun struck the noisy chaos under the bridge to form a rainbow. All so beautiful, as the three of you frolicked in the rain. Bliss.

The Boiling Pot was also great fun. Resting on a rock and watching the constant boisterous meeting of the water, you understood its name. Your mum and Senhor Moutinho stepped from rock to rock the whole time, absorbing everything there was, like overly excited kids, and it stunned you how they seemed to have more energy than you.

Going back to the top was a challenge not only for you and them, but for everybody heedless of size or race. Repeatedly, people would stop, hands on knees, and complain about the steep climb; no wonder the resting places. Some, sweating and looking like they were about to breathe their last, would persuade themselves that it was good for losing weight and for strengthening the heart. Tired and panting, you really wanted to help that stocky man who kept cussing; you wanted to say an encouragement to him, but he looked like he could cuss anything, everything, anyone, so you let him be. Your mum and Senhor Moutinho, ahead of you, urged you to catch up.

Next, you were bungee-jumping from the bridge above the Boiling Pot. She went and came back. He did the same. When your turn came, you understood why they'd screamed like that; you felt gutted, like you'd been condemned to meet your fate in the violent water below. Both cringeworthy and exhilarating. You loved it.

The days that followed saw you visit the Livingstone Museum, the Mukuni Big 5, the Mosi-oa-Tunya National Park, Avani, and Maramba Cultural Village. On Christmas day, you visited the Crocodile Farm and later got a panoramic view of the Zambezi and the Victoria Falls from a helicopter. You ended your tour with a boat cruise on the Zambezi on the 26th.

There was much banter and chatter on the boat. You enjoyed the floating sensation, being so close to the water, and listening to the live band. While most tourists drank wine, whisky, vodka, shandies, and other alcoholic beverages, you drank your orange juice and savoured the feeling of being happy and free. Your mum and Senhor Moutinho would repeatedly check on you and return to their champagne. They looked so good together, dancing and laughing, looking naughtier and happier than anyone.

IV

The drive back home, on the 27th, didn't have the sweet anticipation that had attended the drive down; you could see the lack of enthusiasm in the manner your mum drove, like she didn't want to, almost like she'd done on that morning when Chongo's wife had remained standing, victorious. You sensed sadness from both the front seats and it only compounded your own in the back seat, and it was all because of the funereal and uncertain nature of goodbyes, that you and your mum would be seeing Senhor Moutinho off the next morning at the Kenneth Kaunda International Airport.

V

An arrow pierced your heart the way the plane pierced the sky. It was in that same moment you saw your mum's face crack before it came back together palpably in the realisation he'd be returning soon and everything would be as before.

Back home, you chatted freely with your mum, sharing the highlights of the Livingstone trip, and you both wound up talking about everything because you probably couldn't think of any lowlights. Even what you thought had been a lowlight – times you felt a little invisible – didn't seem like such in retrospect; it seemed now like a time you'd desperately needed to try and find yourself.

You shared with your mum the photos of her and him together that you'd captured on your digital camera. 'Here mum, you looked so happy I've never seen you like this,' you said, showing her a photo of them on the boat.

'Oh yeah,' she said.

When school opened and Senhor Moutinho didn't report back, nor was he still reachable by Skype or any other media, you and your mum didn't know what to think. So unlike him to want to hurt your family. And when your class welcomed the new English Lit teacher, Mr Johnson, whose manner of teaching you found, real or perceived, no different from Mr Lee's, you and your mum, whose pregnancy was on the cusp of the second trimester, were devastated. No one knew what had happened to Senhor Moutinho. The school contacted whoever they could reach, but all of them wondered at his whereabouts.

Still, in your heart, you hoped he'd return one day and take his place in the family and restore your and your mum's happiness. But as the months came and went, you felt your grip on hope weaken, and the supports that held your mum's face in place faltered. Her third trimester came. No show, no word.

Then one morning when the gate opened and the car almost started to kiss the tarmac, a man stood in the light rain, in a black raincoat, his head and eyes under the coat's hood. You didn't pay him attention, but your mum stopped the car and, without one word to you, stepped out and approached him. She stood in much of your line of sight; you couldn't see his face clearly, but you soon realised he was of medium height and build, just like Senhor Moutinho. Your body quivered at the realisation. You stayed put.

'I'm so sorry,' he said. 'I didn't mean to hurt you. For all this time I've been away, yes I deserve the worst. If you take me back, I promise I'll be the best husband in this whole world – your husband.'

When your mum spoke, there was ice in her voice. 'You see I'm very pregnant? Besides, what kind of man leaves his wife for another woman and completely forgets his own child?'

The man was now on his knees. 'A dog – I was a dog but no more. I love you. I've never stopped loving you. Please, my love, take me back.'

Your mum had had enough of this, so she ended it in her own way. 'I'm done with you. Get off your knees, go back to your wife and never return. For as long as I live, I don't want to see your face again.'

Of course the voice was different from Senhor Moutinho's, even the enunciation of words was different, but it was the face that discomfited you; it was the face from the space between awake and asleep, the collage that had intensified since Mr Johnson's arrival. You saw the moustache, the strong jaw and the eyes but they didn't seem angry this time, they appeared sad instead, far away, like something was ebbing from them. And when your mum restarted the engine and drove off, leaving the face farther and farther behind, you felt freed, exorcised.

You thought you saw a little smile tug at her lips, then something returned – yes, life – to her face. Like an octopus, its tentacles touched her every facial feature; and when it was done, it just sat there, on her face, becoming a part of her. Then, for the first time, you saw a sticker she'd posted – she must have done it that very morning – on her side of the dashboard, near the centre. It read: Love is a fire that burns unseen; it's a wound that aches, and yet isn't felt; it's a discontented contentment; it's a pain that rages without hurting.

Acknowledgements

I wish to express my gratitude to several people without whom this work would have remained a dream. To my best friend and wife Christine, the oxygen to my flame, for being the first person to believe in me, read the first drafts – with a smile – and offer constructive criticism. To my little daughters Tukuza and Alisa for not understanding why I would lock myself in the study for hours on end while all you wanted was to play; the resultant ache in my heart gave me focus. To Fay Gadsden for taking time to look at, and believe in, my submission and for facilitating the whole process leading to publication. And to my editor, the indefatigable Nikki Ashley, for helping to fit the dream between these covers.